Infinity of the Bloodlines
Bloodlines

The Legend of Kloth-ee
Begins
K D McManis

Contents

Main Character Genealogy

Eᴌɪᴢᴀᴠᴇᴛʜ Mᴀɢɴᴜs: Daughter of the Leader, scientist, mother of Kloth-ee.

Kloth-ee: Daughter of Elizaveth. She is the holder of the sword of peace that glows bright red and feels like it's on fire. It also glows a bright white in color and feels ice cold when good is around.

Dean: Husband of Elizaveth and stepdad to Kloth-ee. He has dragon wings and arms along with dragon muscles in his legs.

Zaveitth: She is an Ancient Tuathain and leader of her people at the age of thirteen. She sees the past, present, and future and can travel through time with just her mind. She also wrote the laws of time travel as we currently know them.

1
Beginning of Infinity of the bloodlines

L ET ME TAKE YOU back to the past, far back into the past, when the Earth was a newly formed planet and had human life on it. In an ancient spiral galaxy called Celstra, there was an even older planet named Celstra where great and noble beings lived, or so they all thought. I was only a baby of maybe six months when my mother fled the planet riding on a grand-looking white dragon, holding me tightly to her chest to protect me. They fled in a time vortex to the planet called Earth in 2010 to save me, and over the years, the dragon has always been there when we needed it. I may have been born on another planet, but I still have to go to school and learn. I'm called Kloth-ee Magnus, and I'm twelve years old in Earth years; my name has always held some very ancient legacy of power and wisdom that will, in time, be passed down to others. It's not just a mere name but a symbol of the infinite connections to my ancestors and the bloodlines that flow within me. At the tender age of twelve in mortal human years, I stand on the threshold of a journey transcending time and space.

As I navigate the complexities of being a twelve-year-old, I often feel a sense of wisdom beyond my years, a wisdom that whispers of experiences far beyond what my mortal age suggests. My mother and her husband, who I have come to know as my dad, have told me all of the stories of my ancestors that they have come to learn from their time travel journeys. These stories of my ancestors, their triumphs, struggles, and sacrifices, echo in the chambers of my heart and mind, shaping my understanding of the world around me. Every now and again, in the midst of my wanderings, I find myself captivated by the enchanting sight of elves dancing gracefully in the moonlight, their delicate features illuminated by the soft glow of the stars above. With their ethereal beauty and magical presence, these mystical beings never fail to stir my imagination and fill my heart with wonder.

Moreover, the realm of fantasy often extends beyond just elves; fairies, with their shimmering wings and mischievous smiles, flit about in the shadows, casting enchantment spells wherever they go. It is a world where the impossible becomes possible, where dreams take flight and reality is but a distant memory.

But it is not only fantastical creatures that populate my thoughts. In my musings, I have encountered other majestic and powerful dragons whose fiery breath lights up the sky and whose scales gleam like precious gems in the sunlight. Each encounter with these mythical creatures is a reminder of the boundless creativity of the human mind and the endless possibilities that lie beyond our mundane existence.

Beyond the realm of fantasy, I have also forged connections with real, non-magical people from all walks of life. From humble villagers to noble knights, from wise wizards to daring adventurers, each individual I meet brings a unique perspective and a wealth of experiences that enrich my own journey.

my travels have led me to encounter people from other worlds and times, each with their own stories to tell and their own wisdom to impart. Whether it be a time-traveler from the future or an alien from a distant galaxy, the diversity of beings I have met serves as a testament to the infinite variety of existence in the vast tapestry of the universe.

In the intricate tapestry of existence, I find myself weaving threads of past, present, and future, each strand intertwined with the next in a dance of cosmic significance. The realization has dawned upon me that age is but only a number, a fleeting concept in the vast expanse of eternity.

So, as I lay here at the crossroads of time, I embrace all of the infinite possibilities that lie ahead, guided by the bloodlines that course through my veins, connecting me to a heritage as old as the stars themselves. Though I may be young in mortal years, my spirit carries the weight of centuries, a testament to my soon to be legacy. Some speculate that the beginning of time was only a coincidence, yet how did existence come into being? Could it have been an accidental alignment of cosmic forces, a grand design by an unknown creator, or perhaps a complex interplay of quantum mechanics beyond our current comprehension? The question of origins has puzzled philosophers, scientists, and theologians alike for centuries, leading to unlimited theories and beliefs. From the primordial beginning of the ancient Earth to the cosmic dances of galaxies in the vast universes, the tapestry of existence is woven by the threads of mystery and wonder.

Others suggest that divine beings invented time travel to surpass mortals and shape mortality to their liking. In various mythologies and religious traditions, gods, and goddesses are often portrayed as timeless beings who govern the passage of time and shape the destiny of mortals. Whether it's the Norse gods manipulating the threads of fate or the Hindu deities presiding over cycles of creation and destruction, the concept of divine beings controlling time is a recurring theme in human storytelling.

It very well could be the Peace Givers themselves that are trying to shape humanity's world into a world they want and desire. However, since the dawn of time, as humans know it, there have been whispers of one supreme being that even the Gods listen to. A being that is said to hold the incredible and unique ability to see events that are yet to happen have happened and are currently taking place simultaneously. The being has been given a name by humankind, Oracle. This so called Oracle embodies a connection to the unseen forces that shape our reality. Through their visions, they offer a glimpse into the patterns of existence, the flow of time, and the intricate web of causality that binds us together. In their presence, the boundaries of past, present, and future tend to blur, merging into a timeless continuum where all possibilities exist at the same time.

Kloth-ee

As I seem to be lying on the threshold of an unknowing encounter, I'll give you some background on my thoughts. I will tell you about the dreams I've been having lately. My nights have been filled with perplexing dreams that have transported me to different realms throughout time and space, filled with time travel and mystery. In these vivid and real dreams, I constantly encounter a mysterious woman cloaked in a hooded cloak, her enigmatic presence leaving me both intrigued and unsettled. These dream journeys started with the change of seasons to winter, where the air is thick with anticipation, and the distant loud wind heralds the start of a mystical adventure. Each dream unfolds like a chapter in a surreal story, weaving together elements of fantasy and reality in a tapestry of intrigue and wonder.

They always start with me on a distant planet; I'm drawn deeper into the enigmas surrounding the hooded woman and the secrets she holds. This hooded woman always shows up in my dreams just before I make a serious choice. The contrast of familiar elements like summer evenings and snow storms with the fantastical aspects of time travel adds a layer of complexity to these dreams, blurring the lines between what is real and what is imagined. Despite the puzzling nature of these dreams, I find myself unable to tell the difference between my waking hours and my sleeping hours.

In the most recent dream, the hooded woman calls out to me with an outstretched hand. I can hear screaming over her calls as if something terrible will happen. Then, still in my dream state, I'm transported back home while I talk with my parents about my dreams, and they say we should talk to my grandfather, the Leader of the peace giants.

Now, let me take a couple of minutes of your time and fill you in on Dean and my mother. Being only twelve, I, of course, still live with my mom and Dean. For all purposes, I've come to know him as my real dad. My mom, Elizaveth, helped to create this Earth and is the Leader's daughter. She was raised on the planet Celestra and is a Peace Giver. Dean was raised on Earth during this period but is also the son of an ancient Tuathian from the twenty-first dimension. His mother gave him special powers of white dragon wings and arms, along with the leg muscles of a dragon. This is because of a hiking accident that, for some strange reason, caused him to start showing signs of a disease called multiple sclerosis. He still has trouble sleeping at night and walking during the day.

As you can only guess, since you've not seen any signs or proof of time travel, we can travel through time to protect and promote peace. For example, just last week, we traveled back to the ancient civilization of Atlantis to prevent a catastrophic event from occurring; well, we tried anyway. The ability to manipulate time not only allows us to correct past mistakes but also allows us to learn from history and try to shape a possible better future. It is truly a remarkable gift that we must use wisely and responsibly. Transitioning between different periods requires immense skill and concentration, as any misstep could have dire consequences.

As I found myself unwittingly entangled in the Sheriff's web, a middle-aged noble couple, observing the unfolding events from a distance, decided to intervene using their privileged status to gain access to the Sheriff's domain. With a reassuring grip on my arm, the noblewoman swiftly whisked me away from the Sheriff's menacing presence. As we made our daring escape, the nobleman emerged, pursued by a group of the Sheriff's henchmen, urgently urging us to seek refuge in the sheltering embrace of the dense forest.

Taking shelter in the towering trees, the nobleman handed me the mysterious bags, their contents shrouded in secrecy. It wasn't until we felt the threat had dissipated that we dared to inspect the bags, revealing a treasure trove of jewels, gold coins, and riches beyond my wildest imagination. However, our moment of awe was interrupted by the appearance of the less fortunate residents of the forest, the oppressed peasants seeking solace and aid.

Moved by their plight and inspired by a sense of justice, I sought to alleviate their suffering by distributing the wealth bestowed upon me by the noble couple. In that moment, a bond was forged between us, transcending social barriers and uniting us in a common cause. Through this generosity, I earned the respect and friendship of these humble folk, who, in turn, imparted invaluable lessons in combat and cunning upon me.

Under their tutelage, I honed my swordplay, archery, and strategic thinking skills. I learned the art of physical combat and the importance of using words before weapons to pursue peace. In this transformative journey, my identity underwent a profound change, my name evolving from Kloth-ee to the legendary figure of Robbin Hood, a symbol of resistance and compassion in a world plagued by injustice.

Thus, as I navigated the complexities of a world dominated by men, concealing my true identity as a young girl of twelve, I embraced my new mantle as Robbin Hood, defender of the oppressed and beacon of hope in a realm shrouded in darkness. As Robbin Hood, my reputation as a defender of the oppressed and symbol of hope continued to grow throughout the kingdom. Tales of my daring escapades and acts of generosity spread like wildfire, inspiring others to stand up against injustice and tyranny. The oppressed peasants found solace in knowing that someone was fighting for their rights and well-being, instilling a sense of unity and resilience.

With each successful mission to redistribute wealth from the corrupt and powerful to those in need and deserving, my legend grew stronger, painting me as a hero of the common folk and a thorn in the side of the unjust rulers. The nobility, while wary of my actions, couldn't deny the impact I was having on the social fabric of the kingdom, forcing them to reevaluate their positions of privilege and power.

However, as my notoriety increased, so did the threats against me. In his relentless pursuit of capturing me, the Sheriff of Nottingham escalated his efforts to bring about my downfall. His spies lurked in every shadow, his traps becoming more cunning and dangerous daily. Despite the risks, I remained steadfast in my mission, knowing that the cause of justice was worth any personal sacrifice.

Alongside my band of merry outlaws, we continued to outwit the Sheriff's forces, using our wits, skills, and unwavering determination to uphold the values of fairness and compassion. The forest became our sanctuary, a place where the oppressed could find refuge, and our bond as a community grew more robust with each shared victory.

As the sun set on another day in Sherwood Forest, I reflected on the journey that had brought me to this pivotal moment. From a young girl caught amid political turmoil to a legendary figure standing tall against injustice, my transformation was a testament to the power of resilience, courage, and unwavering belief in the possibility of a better world for all. And so, with a bow in hand and a heart filled with resolve, I prepared to face whatever challenges lay ahead, knowing that the spirit of Robbin Hood would endure as a beacon of hope for generations to come.

What I could never have expected to happen, however, was the shocking turn of events where I found myself stealing from my mother. It was a moment of betrayal that I never thought I would experience. Sneaking into the peace talks, amid the dignitaries and delegates, I noticed a distinguished woman seated at the noble peace talks table. Without thinking, I approached her from behind, deftly reaching into her pocket and extracting a small bag. Little did I know that this impulsive act would have such profound consequences.

As I attempted to make my escape, the woman reacted swiftly, seizing my wrist with one hand and pushing back my hood with the other. In that instant, my mother revealed my true identity as I was shown to everyone present, and the expression of shock and disbelief on her face will forever be etched in my memory. The revelation of my actions and the loud accusatory response, calling me out by name. Kloth-ee Magnus. The onlookers, including the noble crowd, immediately branded me as Robin Hood, finally caught in the act of thievery.

The Sheriff, a formidable figure in the room, wasted no time summoning the guards to apprehend me. However, in a surprising twist of events, my mother intervened, aided by her loyal husband, Dean, who courageously stood by her side. With an unwavering voice, she declared that no one would lay a finger on her daughter, emphasizing that my actions were not of my own volition but rather carried out under specific instructions. Her unwavering support and defense in that crucial moment left me both astonished and grateful.

To add to the dramatic scene, the young noble couple I had encountered earlier during my escapade appeared, standing in solidarity with my parents. Their unexpected presence was a testament to the bonds forged amidst the chaos and uncertainty. As the commotion settled and the truth behind my actions began to surface, a sense of unity and understanding permeated the room. Despite the initial turmoil and accusations, the unfolding events ultimately led to a more profound sense of connection and mutual respect among all those involved in this unexpected episode at the peace talks.

From the back of the room, we could see the doors to the grand conference room bang open, and a booming male voice could be heard from everyone present.

"My good friend Elizaveth of the Peace Givers as spoken true to her words. Sheriff if I were you I'd think twice about arresting her daughter. I've known all along what was happening and was with my best wishes that she acted as the Robbin Hood."

With that,t everyone present got to their knee, and my mother and Dean asked him to join them in the peace talks. At that moment, the Sheriff tried to bluff his way out of the trouble he had caused.

"Aw, King Richard! It's exciting that you are alive and with us once again."

"Oh, Sheriff please stop your lies. I know far to well what you have been my people through and that's why I've asked Elizaveth to be present and bring peace to the land once again."

With that, a loud cheer could be heard throughout the kingdom. King Richard made a bold delectation to all his people and said it would always be told from then on.

"The name of Kloth the hood aka Robbin Hood shall always be called Kloth-ee the great. She is a legend in her own time."

The next thing I knew was that the three of us were back in our home. Just as I was waking up from a dream. We stood there quietly, watching what was going to unfold. As I watched myself quickly walking into my parent's room without knocking, I saw Dean just tossing and turning, clearly struggling to fall asleep. It was evident that something was bothering him.

"Dean, can you wake mom up? I need to tell you both something that could be important," I urgently requested.

"No problem," he replied calmly, showing his willingness to help despite being awoken from sleep.

As my mom stirred from her slumber, almost accidentally hitting Dean, she quickly noticed my presence in the dimly lit room. With a concerned expression, she reached over to the bedside lamp and turned it on, illuminating the room.

At that moment, I could see the worry in her eyes as she asked me what was wrong and if I was okay. She was ready to listen and provide the support I needed. The sense of comfort and reassurance that her presence brought was palpable. Taking a deep breath, I explained the situation, knowing that I could trust my family to stand by me no matter what. The atmosphere in the room shifted from one of sleepiness to one of attentiveness and concern.

My mom said this was the most accurate and weirdest dream ever. Going on further, she told me that she would have to ask my grandparents if this dream meant anything and if so. How do we go about finding this hooded, cloaked figure? Dean seemed puzzled since he thought our lives were already complex. In times like these, the importance of family support truly shines through, showing that even in the darkest hours of the night, they are the light that guides us.

At that precise moment, a sense of urgency filled the room, prompting both of my parents to slowly emerge from the comfort of their warm bed and make their way toward the bedroom door.

The eerie atmosphere seemed to have engulfed my parents, rendering them almost robotic in their movements, as if they were mere shadows of their usual selves. It was a perplexing sight, leaving me at a loss for words to describe the peculiar state they found themselves in.

As I turned around to gather my thoughts, I noticed a mysterious figure appearing in a cloud of fog. Clad in a dark, hooded cloak that concealed their features, the silhouette stood ominously outside the bedroom door. The cloak billowed slightly, revealing strands of long hair that escaped from underneath the hood, hinting at the figure's gender. As the cloaked individual loomed over us, the air grew tense with an unspoken unease.

At that moment, a shiver ran down my spine, the realization dawning on me that we were not alone in the room. The silence was deafening, broken only by the faint sound of breathing echoing in the dimly lit space. Who was this mysterious figure, and what intentions lay hidden beneath the cloak? Questions swirled in my mind, each more menacing than the last, as the tension in the room escalated with each passing second. The scene before me felt like a surreal nightmare, with no clear path to discern reality from the eerie illusion surrounding us.

There was still a subtle presence of light fog seeping into the dimly lit room, its source shrouded in mystery. The haze created an atmosphere of intrigue, obscuring much of the surroundings and lending an air of mystique to the scene. Amid the ethereal mist, my gaze fell upon the figure cloaked in secrecy. Despite the limited visibility, I discerned the distinct outline of a sword strapped to their waist, the blade nestled comfortably within its sheath. The sword's hilt peeked through the folds of their cloak, a subtle yet striking detail that hinted at a hidden prowess. The way the sword hung slightly askew added to the enigmatic allure of the figure, evoking a sense of readiness and purpose. At that moment, the room seemed to hold its breath as if anticipating the unfolding of a tale woven with threads of bravery and mystery.

The woman, who appeared to be of a similar age to me, gracefully pulled back her hood with both hands, revealing a warm smile that invited us to follow her. Her outstretched hand signaled for us to accompany her, though she seemed slightly puzzled by my parents' uncharacteristic behavior, reminiscent of zombies in a scenario far from Halloween. Curiosity piqued, I inquired about her name, to which she introduced herself as Zaveitth from the planet Olympus, and she is also a Tuathain. Assuring us there was no rush, she patiently elaborated on various topics and answered my inquiries, shedding light on our surroundings and the unfolding situation. Zaveitth's demeanor exuded a sense of calm guidance, assuring us that we were in capable hands despite the lingering mysteries that surrounded us. As we ventured forward under her guidance, the air hummed with anticipation, each step unraveling new layers of intrigue and discovery.

Zaveitth shared fascinating details about her origins, mentioning that she is what my history would call an Oracle, which holds a significant place in the history of Tuathains and the Peace Givers alike. She explained that she would play a crucial role in establishing the rules and laws of time travel for her people, showcasing her leadership and wisdom. It was intriguing to learn that she inherited this critical position at the young age of thirteen, highlighting her exceptional capabilities and the unique traditions of her society.

Furthermore, Zaveitth hinted at challenges within her family, particularly concerning her father's decisions, which still have long-term repercussions. This revelation added a layer of complexity to her character, showcasing her resilience and determination in the face of adversity. Despite these obstacles, Zaveitth's composure and grace remained unwavering, instilling confidence in us as we delved deeper into the mysteries of her world.

With each passing moment under Zaveitth's guidance, the journey became more enthralling, with every interaction and revelation sparking a sense of wonder and curiosity. Her presence was reassuring and inspiring, leading us toward unknown horizons filled with endless possibilities and revelations. As we continued to follow her through the enigmatic paths of Olympus, it became evident that Zaveitth was not just a guide but a beacon of hope in a realm brimming with secrets and untold stories.

We had crossed far back into time without any devices or time vortex. It was as if we had just walked through a doorway to the past. I wonder if she and I are the same concerning how we travel through time. I'm still new to the idea that time travel exists, but I never thought it was accurate on this level. My parents and I had entered an entirely new and never imagined world by the people of the twentieth century.

The weird thing is that she had no idea when we had traveled back in history to Olympus. I walked over to what I thought was a long walk to the edge of the mountain plateau. While walking to the edge, I noticed numerous open chambers on the ground. I even saw a large body of water that Zaveitth had us stop at, which had a beautiful and clear water pond that she liked to call the nectar of life. There were smooth rocks that we could sit on and rest our feet as we gazed over the pond. We saw some small birds the size of an Earth Hummingbird, dragons talking with people in some weird language, and even, I kid you not, elves and fairies. The last two should not be accurate based on the popular belief of Earth in the year 2025. Yet here they were and, functioning in society.

Zaveitth explained that the pond was a gateway to many different realms, each inhabited by beings beyond our wildest imagination. As we observed the interactions between dragons, elves, fairies, and other mystical creatures, it became evident that our understanding of reality was only limited by the constraints of our earthly perceptions. The harmony and coexistence among these diverse beings challenged our preconceived notions of what was possible, opening our minds to the vast possibilities beyond our known world's boundaries.

Amid the enchanting scenery, Zaveitth shared stories of ancient prophecies and the interconnections of all beings across time and space. The realization dawned upon us that our journey was not merely a physical one but a spiritual awakening to the interconnected web of existence that transcended the confines of our mortal realm. As we sat by the nectar of life, surrounded by magical creatures and ethereal beings, we began to grasp the profound truth that our destinies were intricately woven into the fabric of the universe, guiding us toward a greater purpose yet to be unveiled.

What came next really surprised my mother and I. A beautiful pure white Dragon with the most refined white beard approached us, sitting down and draping its wings over its sides. Dean looked lost and kept asking what he was saying. We told him the dragon spoke English, and Dean told us that's not what he heard. What he was hearing was complete nonsense. That's when Zaveitth said that dragons and Tuathains, along with the Peace Givers by divine right, can understand each other as they speak the same language. She, however, had no explanation for why he could not understand the dragon.

What unfolded before our eyes was beyond any-thing we had ever imagined. With its majestic presence, the white dragon emanated a sense of wisdom and ancient knowledge that tran-scended our understanding. As it communicat-ed with Zaveitth in a language beyond our comprehension, we were left in awe of the mystical connection between beings of different realms. Dean's confusion only deepened our intrigue, highlighting the mysterious ways communication can bridge unknown worlds.

In that moment, a sense of unity washed over us, realizing that the barriers of language and perception were mere illusions in the grand tapestry of existence. The encounter with the dragon reminded us of the boundless possibilities beyond our mundane perceptions, urging us to embrace the unknown with open hearts and minds. As we basked in the dragon's presence, we felt a profound sense of interconnection with all beings, transcending the limitations of ourselves. That moment seemed to be hours in my young mind, but from what we were told, it was only about ten anglapla, which means minute.

Out of nowhere, an elf was running towards Zaveitth and pointing to something in the direction he was running from. She told him to slow down, breathe, and start talking again, but slower than before.

Out of the corner of her eye, Zaveitth noticed a glimmer of light reflecting off something hidden in the dense foliage. Curiosity got the better of her, so she cautiously approached the mysterious object; her senses were on high alert. As she drew closer, the outline of an ancient artifact emerged, its intricate carvings hinting at a forgotten history. The elf's urgent gestures now made sense as he guided Zaveitth to this unexpected discovery, her eyes filled with excitement and caution.

With a sense of reverence, Zaveitth reached out to touch the artifact, feeling a surge of energy coursing through her. The elf's words echoed in her mind, reminding her to approach this newfound treasure with care and respect. As she examined the artifact further, a sense of awe washed over her, realizing that she stood at the threshold of a new adventure that would unravel mysteries long buried in the annals of time.

Guided by the elf's words of wisdom, Zaveitth took a deep breath, allowing the significance of this moment to sink in. With a newfound sense of purpose, she knew this journey was beginning, and the path ahead was filled with challenges and revelations waiting to be uncovered. As the sun dipped below the horizon, casting long shadows across the forest, Zaveitth's determination burned bright, fueled by the promise of discovery and the guidance of our elven companion.

I kept looking at the ancient shiny stone as we walked to where I had no idea. While it kept sending waves of electric shocks through my body, I tried to read the symbols on it. From what Zaveitth told me, they were very ancient Tuathain in their origins, so I could not decipher all of them.

While the ancient piece of shiny stone continued to intrigue me with its mysterious symbols, I couldn't shake off the feeling of being drawn to it. Zaveitth's explanation about the origins of the symbols only added to the enigma surrounding the stone. As we ventured further into the unknown, I couldn't help but wonder about the significance of these ancient Tuathain symbols and what secrets they held. The electric shocks running through my body seemed to intensify, almost guiding us toward a hidden truth waiting to be unveiled.

Lost amid ancient mysteries, I felt a sense of curiosity and a hint of trepidation. The symbols on the stone seemed to whisper stories of a forgotten past, urging me to uncover their meaning. With each step, the energy surrounding the stone grew more robust, as if it led us toward a revelation that could change everything we knew. Despite the uncertainty and the unknown dangers ahead, I felt a surge of determination to unravel the secrets hidden within the ancient symbols.

As we delved deeper into the ancient realm of Tuathain, the stone's power seemed to resonate with my very being, awakening a sense of connection to a long-lost civilization. The journey ahead was filled with challenges and uncertainties. Still, the allure of the mysterious stone and its cryptic symbols propelled us forward, driven by a thirst for knowledge and a desire to uncover the truth buried beneath centuries of history.

As we approached the heart of the ancient Tuathain civilization, the stone's symbols seemed to pulse with newfound energy, as if re-acting to our presence. The air around us crack-led with anticipation, and a sense of urgency filled the atmosphere, driving us deeper into the mysteries surrounding us. Each step we took echoed the weight of history, with the promise of unlocking secrets long forgotten by time.

The enigmatic symbols on the stone appeared to shift and change, almost as if responding to our quest for knowledge. It was as though the stone itself was a living entity, guiding us toward a revelation that held the key to unraveling the mysteries of the past. The connection between the symbols and our journey grew stronger, in-tertwining our fates with the ancient civilization that had left its mark on the land.

With each passing moment, the allure of the stone and its cryptic symbols intensified, fueling our determination to uncover the truth hidden within their intricate designs. The path ahead was fraught with challenges and uncertainties. Still, the pull of the ancient mysteries was irre-sistible, drawing us ever closer to a revelation that promised to reshape our understanding of history. Amid the unknown, we found ourselves bound by a shared purpose – to decipher the secrets of the past and unlock the power of the ancient symbols. The ancient stone's symbols continued to mesmerize us, their enigmatic nature drawing us deeper into the heart of the Tuathain civilization. As we delved further into the labyrinth of mysteries, the sense of urgency grew, compelling us to unravel the secrets hidden within the intricate designs. Each twist and turn in the path echoed with the whispers of history, urging us to uncover the truth that had been veiled for centuries.

The pulsating energy of the symbols seemed to guide our every move, leading us toward a revelation that held the power to reshape our understanding of the past. The connection between us and the ancient civilization felt palpable as if we were bound by a shared destiny to decipher the cryptic messages etched in stone. With determination fueling our steps, we pressed on, undeterred by the challenges that lay ahead.

As the mysteries unfolded before us, the allure of the ancient symbols only intensified, fueling our curiosity and resolve. The journey toward enlightenment was fraught with obstacles, but the promise of unlocking the power of the symbols kept us steadfast in our quest. Amid uncertain unity, a sense of purpose united us, driving us towards a revelation that would unlike all of the ancient wisdom of the Tuathain civilization.

2
The Forgotten Fortress

IN THE DISTANCE, WE could see a large gate towering far above a large tower. Zaveitth had never heard of this place before and thought it best to practice precautions further. The artifact kept pushing me towards that old scary gate that turned out to be a large fortress. It was complete with a castle that once appeared to be the area's crown jewel. Now, it was only falling into ruins and crumbling to pieces. Zaveitth stopped us by putting her arm before me while she spoke.

"I've only seen this place in my dreams, but never gave it any further thought till now."

"I agree with you. I thought it was just a dream after watching a fantasy adventure movie." I replied

The fortress stood as a silent sentinel of a long gone era, its walls echoing with whispers of forgotten tales and lost glory. Zaveitth's eyes scanned the crumbling stones, each a testament to the passage of time and the inevitable decay of all things. The artifact pulsed in my hand, urging me to explore further, to unravel the mysteries hidden within the fortress's ancient walls.

As we cautiously made our way through the overgrown courtyard, a sense of foreboding hung heavy in the air. Zaveitth's grip on my arm tightened a silent warning to proceed cautiously once the majestic castle loomed before us, its turrets reaching toward the sky like skeletal fingers clawing at the clouds.

"I feel like we're stepping into a forgotten legend," Zaveitth whispered, her voice barely audible above the rustling of the wind through the dilapidated towers. I nodded in agreement, the weight of centuries pressing down on us like a heavy cloak.

With each step we took, the fortress revealed more secrets, each chamber holding echoes of a long forgotten past. As we delved deeper into the castle's heart, I couldn't shake the feeling that we were not alone and that the ghosts of the past walked beside us, guiding our path through the labyrinthine corridors.

And as we finally reached the inner sanctum, a sense of awe washed over us. Before us lay the artifact's true purpose, a relic of unimaginable power lost to time. Zaveitth's eyes shone with fear and excitement, her hand reaching out to touch the artifact that had led us on this incredible journey.

Together, we stood on the precipice of discovery, ready to unlock the secrets of the fortress and uncover the truth hidden within its ancient stones. As we stood in awe before the artifact, its ancient power seemed to hum in the air around us, a palpable energy that sent shivers down our spines. Zaveitth's fingers trembled as she reached to touch the artifact, her eyes reflecting reverence and trepidation. The fortress's secrets lay before us, waiting to be unraveled, waiting for us to unlock the mysteries buried beneath centuries of dust and neglect.

With a shared glance, we knew that we were on the cusp of something extraordinary that would change our lives forever. The artifact pulsed with a faint light as if urging us to delve deeper into its origins, to uncover the truth that had been hidden for so long. The weight of responsibility settled on our shoulders, a realization that we were the chosen ones to reveal the fortress's long-forgotten legacy.

Beings who transcended the limitations of mortal life to touch the very essence of creation. The cosmic forces that pulsed through the chamber beckoned us to explore further, to seek out the truths hidden in the fortress's depths. As we basked in the celestial light that bathed the chamber, we knew that our journey was far from over, for the mysteries of the cosmos held infinite possibilities for those willing to embrace the unknown.

A ghostly figure was very dressed in what appeared to be the throne room. Perhaps he had been some royal leader in his day. He was talking in the ancient tongue of the Tuathains. He went on and on about his son, who had made some bad choices, so the Oracle of the time turned him into the very first elf.

The ghostly king even said that Zaveitth and I were never meant to be in the same period. We each have our mission in life. Here's the thing: we both somehow knew that he would say that. However, He tried to grab that shiny object he still held onto. He told us that it is only a tiny pietiny and that it is the entire big object it goes to.

He emphasized that the shiny object was a crucial part of a giant puzzle that needed to be solved. As we stood there, captivated by his words, the ghostly king's presence seemed to grow stronger, almost as if he was trying to convey a sense of urgency.

Despite the cryptic nature of his message, an undeniable sense of purpose lingered in the air. Zaveitth and I exchanged knowing glances, silently acknowledging the task's weight ahead of us.

The king's words echoed in our minds as we contemplated the significance of the shiny object and its connection to the mysterious big object he spoke of. It was clear that our paths had crossed for a reason and that unraveling this enigma would require us to work together in harmony.

With a newfound sense of determination, we set out on our journey, knowing that the fate of our lives and perhaps the entire world rested on our ability to decipher the secrets hidden within the objects that lay before us.

Dean and I decided to explore the castle further, intrigued by the mysteries it held within its ancient walls. We stumbled upon a hidden chamber filled with old books and dusty artifacts as we wandered through the dimly lit corridors. We found a map among the relics that seemed to lead to a hidden treasure buried deep within the castle grounds. Excitement filled the air as we realized the adventure ahead of us.

My mother, Elizaveth, joined us in deciphering the map, her eyes sparkling with curiosity and determination. It became clear that she knew about the object we possessed, hinting at its significance in unlocking the secrets of the castle's past. With her guidance, we embarked on a quest to unravel the mysteries of the ancient artifact and uncover the truth behind its enigmatic powers.

As we delved deeper into the castle's history, we encountered cryptic symbols, puzzling riddles, and hidden passageways that tested our wit and courage. Each discovery brought us closer to unraveling the secrets guarded for centuries. With every step we took, the bond between Dean, my mother, and I grew stronger, united by our shared determination to uncover the truth and protect the legacy of the castle.

Together, we faced challenges, overcame obstacles, and forged unforgettable memories in our quest for knowledge and adventure. The castle became more than just a place to stay for the night; it became a symbol of our shared journey, a testament to our resilience, and a reminder that the greatest treasures are often found in the most unexpected places.

When we started to go down an old spooky tunnel in that castle, a strange little creature came out of one of the cracks in the walls. The creature had glowing eyes that seemed to pierce through the tunnel's darkness, sending shivers down our spines. Its movements were quick and erratic, making it difficult to discern its proper form. As it hurried past us, we could hear faint whispers echoing off the damp walls, adding to the eerie atmosphere. The encounter left us both intrigued and unsettled, wondering what other secrets lay within the castle's depths. We decided to keep going despite that weird and strange encounter.

We cautiously proceeded further into the tunnel's depths, our footsteps echoing off the stone walls. The dim light filtering in through cracks in the ceiling cast eerie shadows around us, heightening our sense of unease. The ancient stones seemed to whisper tales of long-forgotten secrets, adding to the mysterious aura of the place. Despite the strange encounter with the mysterious creature, our curiosity remained unquenched, propelling us to uncover more of the castle's mysteries.

The air grew colder and heavier as we ventured deeper, each step heavier than the last. It was as if the weight of history bore down on us, urging us to delve further into the unknown. Suddenly, a faint sound reached our ears, a soft rustling that seemed to come from the shadows ahead. We strained our eyes to see what lay beyond, but the darkness obscured our vision, leaving us to rely on our other senses to navigate the eerie passageways.

The earlier whispers grew louder, swirling around us like a sinister melody. Goosebumps prickled on our skin as we pressed on, deter-mined to unravel the mysteries hidden within the ancient walls. Our hearts beat in anticipa-tion as we rounded a corner, a faint glimmer catching our attention. Illuminated by a faint light, we discovered a hidden chamber filled with ancient artifacts and dusty tomes, each holding a piece of the castle's enigmatic past.

The air in the chamber was thick with the scent of old parchment and decay, adding to the eerie ambiance of the place. Each artifact seemed to hold a story waiting to be told, a piece of histo-ry waiting to be uncovered. Despite the chilling atmosphere and the unsettling encounters, our sense of adventure grew stronger. We were like modern-day explorers, delving into the castle's depths in search of its long-buried truths.

We knew that within the castle's depths lay untold secrets and mysteries waiting to be unveiled. The thrill of discovery mingled with the fear of the unknown, creating a heady mix of emotions that spurred us forward. The ancient stones whispered their secrets, the shadows danced with hidden truths, and we, the intrepid explorers, were determined to uncover them all. No matter what eerie encounters awaited us in the labyrinthine corridors, our thirst for knowledge and adventure would not be quenched until every mystery was unraveled.

In that time and in that area of the castle, Zaveitth told us she better go and find which of her people could help with all of these discoveries. I mean, we had a lot of old and ancient relics, old scrolls, and jewels. She then left just after arriving at our house without a trace. My mom looked through some of the ancient relics and scrolls. They were older than her and in the most ancient tongues of the ancient Tuathains. The creature we had encountered earlier came through one of the cracks in the walls. The crack was at my chest level, so I could see this creature as it introduced itself as a derbwarey.

The derbwarey said we were the first beings within those castle walls for millions of years. The great leader was the last being to walk those halls, now a ghost of himself.

The derbwarey continued explaining that the ancient leader had left behind powerful artifacts hidden within the castle's walls. These artifacts held immense knowledge and magic that could only be unlocked by those deemed worthy. As the derbwarey guided us through the corridors, we stumbled upon a hidden chamber filled with glowing crystals that emitted a soothing aura. It whispered tales of forgotten legends and mysteries waiting to be unraveled.

Intrigued by the secrets hidden within the castle, we delved deeper into its depths, uncovering chambers filled with mystical relics and ancient texts written in long-forgotten languages. The derbwarey revealed that these artifacts were vital to understanding the land's history and lost civilizations. Each artifact told a story of a bygone era, vividly depicting the struggles and triumphs of those who came before us.

As we delved deeper into our exploration, we were met with many fascinating creatures similar to the derbwarey, each a custodian of a fragment of the castle's rich history. These beings regaled us with captivating accounts of ancient battles waged, alliances forged in the crucible of conflict, and the ebb and flow of empires long lost to the annals of time. The very stones of the castle seemed imbued with spectral energy, resonating with the echoes of bygone eras when magic and enigma held sway over the land.

Our expedition into the heart of this venerable fortress unfolded like a tapestry of forgotten lore, each step unearthing new revelations about the enigmatic world concealed within its formidable walls. At this juncture, Zaveitth, accompanied by her people, rejoined our company, her people equally astounded by the clandestine existence of this ancient stronghold. Scholars expressed bafflement at the absence of any historical record about this mysterious castle, raising more questions than answers.

The diverse derbwareys of the castle assembled around us, eager to impart their wisdom and cautionary tales, yet our attention remained fixated on the wondrous sights unfolding before us. Unbeknownst to us, amidst their earnest attempts to communicate a foreboding message about the repercussions of removing anything from the castle, we remained oblivious to their subtle warnings. Little did we realize the gravity of their words and the potential consequences that loomed ominously over the land should we disregard their warnings.

None of us knew how to get back to the main entrance of the forgotten fortress, though. We decided to split up and search for clues that might lead us back to the main entrance of the forgotten fortress. Some of us explored the dimly lit corridors, while others scoured the dusty rooms for any signs of a way out. As we delved deeper into the maze-like structure, the sense of being lost only grew stronger.

Despite our best efforts, the layout of the fortress seemed to defy logic, with twisting passages and hidden chambers that confounded our attempts to navigate our way back. Every step we took felt like a step further into the unknown, and the shadows cast by the flickering torches played tricks on our minds.

As time passed, a sense of unease settled over the group. The realization that we might be trapped in this ancient place weighed heavily on our spirits. We knew we had to find a way out before darkness fell and the fortress became even more foreboding. The urgency of our situation spurred us on, driving us to search every nook and cranny for a possible escape route.

The four of us, including Zaveitth, Dean, our mom, and myself, successfully ascended a series of winding stairs that led us to another level of the structure we were exploring. Along the way, we stumbled upon a window that allowed us to gaze outside. Through the window, our eyes beheld a breathtaking sight - what appeared to be a vast expanse resembling a majestic mountain. Zaveitth, with her insightful knowledge, suggested that this intriguing discovery might be the long-lost Ancient Tuathains' Celestra castle.

As we stood there, marveling at the mysterious mountain structure before us, our minds began to wander, envisioning the tales and legends that might be associated with such a place. The possibility of exploring the depths of history and uncovering ancient secrets filled us with excitement and curiosity. Zaveitth's mention of the Celestra castle sparked a sense of wonder, igniting a desire to learn more about the fabled Tuathains and their enigmatic civilization.

Intrigued by the prospect of unraveling the mysteries shrouding the Celestra castle, we eagerly discussed our next steps. Should we venture further to get a better knowledge of the castle? Or perhaps research the history of the Tuathains to gain a deeper understanding of this remarkable discovery? The air was thick with anticipation as we pondered the endless possibilities ahead.

With each passing moment, the ancient aura of the Celestra castle seemed to beckon us, inviting us to delve into its secrets and unlock the hidden truths that lay dormant within its walls. Our journey to this point had been nothing short of exhilarating, and we knew that the adventure had only just begun. As we gazed out the window again, the castle silhouette against the horizon seemed to whisper tales of a bygone era, urging us to embark on a quest for knowledge and discovery. And so, with hearts full of anticipation and minds brimming with curiosity, we prepared to uncover the mysteries of the Celestra castle and the lost Ancient Tuathains.

3
Celestra Castle's Secretes

L OOKING AROUND THE ROOM we were in, I first landed on a magnificent four-poster bed adorned with ancient, tattered drapes cascading from the top posts. The bed, once a symbol of opulence and grandeur, now stood as a testament to the passage of time and the wear of history. The faded fabric of the drapes whispered stories of nights spent under their shelter, tales of dreams woven within their threads. The intricate carvings on the bedposts hinted at a craftsmanship long forgotten, a skill passed down through generations.

I couldn't help but imagine the countless souls resting on its creaking frame as I gazed at the bed. Perhaps it had cradled a weary traveler seeking refuge from a storm or a lovesick poet penning verses of longing in the dim candlelight. The layers of dust that had settled on its surface seemed to silence the echoes of laughter and tears that once filled the room.

The room itself exuded an air of faded elegance. A chandelier, its crystals dulled with age, hung from the ceiling like a forgotten memory. The worn wooden floorboards creaked underfoot, bearing witness to the passage of time.

Time seemed to stand still in this room, capturing moments of joy and sorrow within its walls. Each piece of furniture, each crack in the plaster, told a story of a life once lived. As I stood there, surrounded by the whispers of the past, I couldn't help but feel a sense of reverence for the history that lingered in the air. It was in this very room that we witnessed a marvelous site. One that we had never seen before or after that. A woman just appeared, and Zaveitth gasped with a surprised look on her face.

The woman spoke after a few minutes of silence. I'm guessing that she was trying to figure out where and when she was. She said her name was Marlanaveth unless we promised to bring peace to the world. She would turn that good looking man, who, to clarify, was Dean. She would turn him into a fourteen year old boy. We felt like we couldn't make that promise only since everyone who lives and has lived before us has the right and privilege to choose right from wrong on their own, hoping that I would learn something either way about it.

So we made our choice and hoped for all the best.

In the aftermath of our decision, the room seemed to hold its breath as if waiting for the repercussions of our choice to unfold. Marlanaveth's piercing gaze bore into our souls, a mix of disappointment and understanding flickering in her eyes. The air grew heavy with the weight of our decision, each heartbeat echoing in the silence that enveloped us.

As Dean stood there, the threat of transformation hanging over him like a dark cloud, I couldn't shake the feeling of uncertainty that gnawed at my insides. Would our refusal to make the promise condemn us to a fate worse than we could imagine? Or would it be the catalyst for a new path fraught with challenges and revelations?

Once a sanctuary of faded elegance and whispered histories, the room now felt charged with an energy that crackled in the air. The dust motes danced in the dim light, casting shadows that whispered secrets of what was to come. The chandelier above swayed imperceptibly as if caught in a breeze that only it could feel.

Amid this tense atmosphere, Marlanaveth's voice broke through the silence, her words carrying a weight that settled in the marrow of our bones. She spoke of prophecies and destinies intertwined, of choices made and consequences faced. And as we stood there on the precipice of uncertainty, I knew that whatever lay ahead would test us in ways we could never have imagined.

The tension in the room was comparable, like a storm brewing on the horizon, ready to unleash its fury. Marlanaveth's presence seemed to warp reality, her words echoing in the chamber like a haunting melody. Dean's fate hung in the balance, a fragile thread that could snap at any moment, plunging us into an unknown abyss. As we stood there, paralyzed by the gravity of our decision, the weight of responsibility pressed down upon us like a heavy cloak.

The air crackled with anticipation, each heartbeat a drumbeat of uncertainty. Would our choice lead us down a path of redemption or damnation? The room, once a sanctuary of faded elegance, now felt like a battleground where destinies clashed and intertwined. Shadows danced across the walls, whispering secrets of what was to come, their cryptic messages adding to the foreboding in the air.

Amid this charged atmosphere, I couldn't help but wonder about the true nature of Marlanaveth's request. Was it a test of our moral fiber, a trial to prove our worthiness? Or was it a prelude to a more significant conflict, one that would shape the course of history itself? As the silence stretched between us, I braced myself for the unknown, ready to face whatever challenges lay ahead with courage and determination.

With that, Marlanaveth's voice spiked in its tone as she spoke. She was chanting in that old Tuathain language. Dean's dragon wings and arms started disappearing, followed by his facial hair. My mother was trying to hold his hand as he was screaming in pain. He began to get shorter and soon became a fourteen-year-old boy with all of his memories from his adult life. He lay there on the floor crying from all of the pain his whole body just went through.

In the aftermath of Dean's transformation, the room seemed to hold its breath, the tension thick in the air like a tangible presence. Marlanaveth's gaze bore into us, a mix of disappointment and resignation in her eyes. The weight of our decision hung heavy upon us, each heartbeat a reminder of the gravity of our choice.

A sense of unease settled over the room as Dean lay there, now a fourteen-year-old boy with the memories of his entire life intact. The shadows danced on the walls, whispering of the consequences of our actions. The chandelier above swayed gently, casting a dim light on the scene unfolding before us.

Marlanaveth's chanting in the ancient Tuathain language echoed through the chamber, the words resonating with power and mystery. Dean's transformation was a stark reminder of the forces at play, the boundaries between reality and myth blurring before our eyes.

As we grappled with the aftermath of our choice, a sense of foreboding lingered in the air. The room, once a sanctuary of faded elegance and whispered histories, now bore witness to a pivotal moment that would shape our destinies. The weight of responsibility pressed down upon us, urging us to confront the challenges ahead with courage and resolve.

Amid uncertainty and transformation, we stood on the threshold of a new chapter, where prophecies and choices intertwined in a tapestry of fate. The room, now charged with an energy that crackled in the air, seemed to pulse with the echoes of a past long forgotten and a future yet to be written. As Marlanaveth's incantations faded into the ether, a sense of anticipation filled the room, mingling with the remnants of ancient magic that lingered in the air. Dean's transformation marked a turning point in our journey, merging past and present that defied conventional understanding. The threads of destiny intertwined around us, weaving a complex tapestry of choices and consequences to shape the path ahead.

The flickering candlelight cast shifting shadows on the walls, mirroring the uncertainty that clouded our minds. Each whispered word, each hesitant breath, carried the weight of the unknown, a reminder of the fragility of our existence in the face of forces beyond our control. As we stood on the precipice of change, the room seemed to hold its breath once more, bracing for the impact of what was yet to come.

In the silence that followed, a sense of unity emerged, a shared understanding that our fates were bound together in ways we had yet to comprehend. The echoes of Marlanaveth's ritual lingered in the corners of the chamber, a haunting melody that spoke of secrets long buried and truths waiting to be revealed. As we gazed into the uncertain future, a spark of determination ignited within us, a silent promise to face whatever challenges awaited with unwavering resolve. The soft glow of the candles continued to illuminate the room, casting a warm yet mysterious ambiance that enveloped us in a cocoon of anticipation. As Marlanaveth's words faded into the ether, a sense of unity and purpose lingered among us, binding our fates together in ways we had never imagined. The intricate dance of destiny unfolded before our eyes, revealing a tapestry of interconnected paths that led us toward an uncertain future.

In the stillness that followed, the echoes of ancient magic whispered secrets of forgotten lore, hinting at the challenges and revelations that awaited us on our journey. Each breath seemed to resonate with the weight of the unknown, a reminder of the fragile balance between choice and fate that governed our lives. As we stood on the threshold of transformation, a newfound sense of determination ignited within us, fueling our spirits with the resolve to confront whatever trials lay ahead.

The shadows danced on the walls, mirroring the complexities of our intertwined destinies, while the flickering candlelight symbolized the flicker of hope that burned within us. With each heartbeat, we embraced the uncertainty of the future, knowing that the threads of our lives were woven together in a tapestry of shared experiences and destinies. As we prepared to step into the unknown, we did so with a sense of unity and purpose, ready to face whatever challenges the weaving of fate had in store for us.

We then heard the roar of a dragon, but was it the white dragon we had met earlier in our journey? We ran out of the room and looked for a balcony close by. We finally found one and stood out on that balcony watching the white dragon and what appeared to be a red with black two headed dragon fighting in the air. The red with black dragon was spitting its yellow fire breath at the white dragon, but it dodged the reaction from the white dragon.

The clash of the dragons in the sky was a spectacle unlike any other. The white dragon, majestic and powerful, soared through the air with grace and determination, evading the fiery breath of the red and black two headed dragon. The sky above the ancient castle was illuminated by flame and flashes of lightning, creating a scene of epic proportions as we stood on the balcony, transfixed by the battle unfolding before us; a sense of awe and wonder washed over us. The dragons' roars echoed through the night, shaking the very foundations of the earth.

The white dragon, with its shimmering scales and piercing eyes, seemed to give an aura of purity and strength, while the red and black dragon emanated a sense of chaos and power with its menacing appearance and dual heads. The two adversaries clashed in a dance of fire and fury, their movements fluid and precise, each trying to gain the upper hand in the fierce aerial combat. As the battle raged on, the castle below trembled with the force of their clashes, the very stones seeming to vibrate with the intensity of the duel. Amid this epic confrontation, a sense of Certainty hung in the air, as if the battle's outcome had been written in the stars. The fate of the dragons seemed intertwined with our own, their struggle mirroring the challenges and conflicts that lay ahead on our journey. As we watched in awe, the dragons' battle became a symbol of the larger forces in the world, a reminder of the eternal struggle between light and darkness, good and evil.

The white dragon's wings beat against the night sky, creating a whirlwind of energy that crackled with power. The red and black dragon, undeterred by the fierceness of its opponent, continued to unleash torrents of flame, each blast illuminating the darkness with a fiery glow. The clash of elements, fire against ice, rage against serenity, painted a vivid picture of the eternal struggle for balance in the world.

While that red and black dragon tried to claw the white dragon's wings off with its very sharp claws, the white dragon was trying to bite at its neck and stop it. Finally, Zaveitth yelled at the top of her lungs.

"In the name of the great Tuathains! You will stop this fighting right now!"

The command echoed through the night sky, cutting through the chaos of the dragon's battle like a sharp blade. Zaveitth's voice carried a weight that seemed to still the very air around us, commanding attention and respect. As her words hung in the air, a moment of silence descended upon the scene, the dragons pausing in their fierce combat to regard the source of the powerful proclamation.

The white dragon, wings outstretched in a display of dominance, turned its gaze towards Zaveitth, a look of recognition flickering in its eyes. The red and black two-headed dragon, its fiery breath momentarily extinguished, seemed to hesitate in the face of the ancient Tuathain's authority. The clash of elements, fire and ice, chaos and order, reached a temporary ceasefire as the dragons acknowledged the presence of a force greater than themselves.

In the aftermath of Zaveitth's command, a sense of calm settled over the balcony, the tension in the air dissipating like mist in the morning sun. The dragons, once locked in a battle of wills and power, now stood still, their eyes closed in a silent exchange of understanding. The night sky, illuminated by the fading remnants of their fiery clash, bore witness to a moment of unexpected peace amid the storm of conflict.

As we watched in awe, the dragons' postures shifted, a subtle indication of a truce forged in the le. The white dragon, with its regal demeanor and unwavering gaze, seemed to convey a sense of respect towards Zaveitth, while the red and black dragon, its fiery eyes softened by a glimmer of acquiescence, mirrored a newfound willingness to heed her words. The balance of power had shifted, not towards domination or submission, but towards a mutual understanding of the forces in their ancient dance of destiny.

With a final nod of approval from Zaveitth, the dragons unfurled their wings and took to the sky again, this time in a synchronized flight that spoke of unity rather than conflict. The night air hummed with anticipation as if the fabric of reality had shifted in response to the ancient Tuathain's intervention. As the dragons soared into the darkness, their silhouettes blending into the starlit canvas above, we were left with a profound sense of wonder at the mysteries that lay beyond the veil of our understanding.

The one thing we never really honestly expected to happen did happen. A bright yellow and white light surrounded both Zaveitth and I. At the same time, Dean was lifted about ten feet above the floor on a cloud of the same color. My grandfather, the leader himself, then appeared beside my grandmother. With the look of love in their eyes, my grandfather spoke.

"Dean, it's so good to see you again, and I must say the years have been very kind to you. You look younger, and you're not currently dealing with the disease of multiple sclerosis. You have suffered hard and long days these last couple of years. We all knew it wouldn't be forever when your mother gave you those special powers.

My intelligent and lovely granddaughter Kloth-ee, I see you have found a new friend in Zaveitth. You will soon notice that your powers of seeing the past, present, and future are in your consent mind. These are the gifts to people so they can continue to help bring peace to the world throughout time and space."

Before anyone else could say or do anything, another light show started to display. A show of dark orange and dark red while figures began walking out of it.

The figures emerging from the display of dark orange and dark red lights were unlike anything we had ever seen. Their presence exuded an aura of ancient wisdom and power as if they were beings from a realm beyond our comprehension. As they approached, reverence and trepidation washed over us, mingling with the residual energy of the dragons' battle that lingered in the air.

The leader of the mysterious figures, a tall and imposing figure with eyes that seemed to hold the secrets of the universe, spoke in a voice that resonated with authority and ageless knowledge. "Greetings, travelers of time and space," he began, his words carrying a weight that seemed to echo through the very fabric of reality. "You have been chosen to embark on a journey of great importance, one that will test your courage, wisdom, and resolve."

Beside him stood a figure cloaked in shadows, her presence both comforting and unsettling. Her eyes, pools of infinite depth and mystery, seemed to pierce through the veils of time and space, revealing glimpses of past, present, and future intertwined in a complex tapestry of fate. "Welcome, young ones," she whispered, her voice a melodic blend of ancient tongues. "The threads of destiny have brought you here, to this pivotal moment where choices will shape the course of worlds."

As we stood in awe of these enigmatic beings, a sense of purpose and destiny settled upon us, binding our fates to the unfolding events with an unbreakable bond. The leader extended a hand towards us, offering guidance and strength in facing the challenges ahead. "Embrace your gifts, for they are the keys to unlocking the mysteries of the cosmos," he intoned, his gaze penetrating our very souls.

With a silent nod of acceptance, we stepped forward, ready to embark on a journey that would transcend time and space, leading us toward a destiny written in the stars. The figures around us shimmered with ethereal light, their forms shifting and merging with the universe's energies. And as we took our first steps toward the unknown, a sense of unity and purpose filled our hearts, guiding us toward a future where the boundaries between reality and myth would blur once more. The ethereal beings led us through a shimmering portal that transcended the limits of our known reality, transporting us to a realm where time and space intertwined in a dance of cosmic proportions. As we emerged into this new dimension, a sense of wonder and awe enveloped us, the air pulsating with the energy of ancient starlight.

The landscape before us was a tapestry of swirling galaxies and celestial bodies, each shining with a brilliance that defied description. The leader of the beings turned to us, his eyes alight with the wisdom of eons past, and gestured towards the horizon where a constellation of shimmering stars beckoned us forward.

"We stand at the threshold of the great cosmic tapestry," he spoke, his voice resonating with the harmony of the universe. "Each star, each planet, each nebula holds a story waiting to be unraveled, a truth waiting to be discovered. It is your destiny to journey through the cosmos, to seek out the mysteries that lie beyond the veil of perception."

Beside him, the cloaked figure stepped forward, her presence a soothing balm to our senses. "The celestial realms are a reflection of the inner workings of the soul," she whispered, her words weaving a melody that echoed through the vast expanse. "As you traverse the galaxies and traverse the depths of your being, remember that the answers you seek are not merely out there, but within."

With newfound resolve and a sense of purpose burning in our hearts, we ventured into the unknown, guided by the light of a million stars and the whispers of cosmic winds. The journey ahead promised challenges and revelations beyond our wildest dreams. Still, we embraced it with open hearts, ready to embrace the infinite possibilities that awaited us in the boundless expanse of the cosmos. The cosmic winds whispered secrets of the universe as we journeyed through the vast expanse of the celestial realms. Each star we passed held a story of creation and destruction, birth and rebirth, echoing the eternal cycle of life itself. The constellations above guided our path, their patterns intricately woven like threads in the fabric of time.

As we delved deeper into the cosmic tapestry, we encountered beings of light and shadow, each offering wisdom and challenges to test our resolve. The trials we faced mirrored the inner struggles of our souls, pushing us to confront our fears and embrace our strengths. Through the trials, we discovered hidden truths about ourselves, unlocking the dormant potential.

The journey through the cosmos was not just a physical voyage but a spiritual awakening, a quest to understand the interconnections of all things. We learned that the universe was not separate from us but a part of us, a reflection of our deepest desires and fears. In the boundless expanse of the cosmos, we found unity in diversity, harmony in chaos, and beauty in the unknown.

With stardust in our veins and the echoes of cosmic melodies in our hearts, we continued our odyssey through the stars, forever changed by the revelations that awaited us in the infinite reaches of the universe. As we ventured into the cosmic unknown, the stars whispered tales of ancient civilizations that once thrived among the galaxies. Their remnants scattered across the universe, leaving traces of their wisdom and legacy for those who dared to seek them. We encountered celestial ruins adorned with symbols of forgotten languages, hinting at a profound connection between past and present.

Amidst the cosmic ruins, we encountered celestial beings of pure energy, guardians of cosmic knowledge and wisdom. They bestowed visions of the universe's creation, revealing the intricate dance of heavenly bodies that shaped the cosmos. Through their guidance, we glimpsed the threads of destiny that intertwined our fates with the cosmic tapestry, binding us to the eternal cycle of existence.

As we delved deeper into the mysteries of the cosmos, we discovered the cosmic symphony that resonated through the void, a harmonious blend of light and darkness, creation and destruction. Each celestial note carried the essence of cosmic truths, unveiling the interconnections of all things in the vast expanse of space. We embraced the cosmic melodies, letting them guide us through the cosmic labyrinth toward enlightenment and understanding.

With newfound knowledge and cosmic insights, we embarked on a journey beyond the stars, transcending the boundaries of time and space. The echoes of cosmic melodies continued reverberating within us, igniting a spark of cosmic consciousness that illuminated our path through the infinite reaches of the universe. In the cosmic dance of creation and rebirth, we found solace in the eternal symphony of the cosmos, forever bound to the cosmic winds that whispered secrets of the universe.

4
Struggles Among the Cosmos

THE FIRST PLANET WE arrived on was none other than Olympus. Zaveitth said it looked much different, even newer if she could say that. It did look like it might have looked long before she had been there. The strange figures were still with us, and they had removed their hoods. The female was me, but a lot older, at least twenty years older.

The figures stood before us, their presence commanding attention. A sense of familiarity washed over me as they removed their hoods, revealing their true identities. Standing there, the older version of myself was a glimpse into a possible future. It was as if time had folded upon itself, showing me a path that could be taken. The realization hit me that our journey to Olympus was not just physical but a trip through time and self-discovery.

The landscape of Olympus seemed to shift and change with each passing moment, mirroring the inner transformations we were experiencing. The air was filled with a sense of mystery and ancient wisdom as if the very essence of the planet held secrets waiting to be unveiled. Zaveitth's words echoed in my mind, reminding me that perception could be a powerful tool in shaping our reality.

As we ventured further into the heart of Olympus, I couldn't help but wonder about the significance of our encounter with the figures. Were they guardians of this realm, guiding us toward a deeper understanding of ourselves? Or were they reflections of our inner struggles and desires manifesting in physical form? The answers eluded me, but one thing was certain – our journey had only begun, and the mysteries of Olympus were far from being unraveled. The path ahead seemed to twist and turn, leading us deeper into the heart of Olympus. Each step we took resonated with a sense of purpose as if the ground beneath our feet guided us toward a greater understanding. The whispers of the wind carried fragments of ancient tales, hinting at the rich history hidden within these sacred grounds.

As we delved further into the mysteries of Olympus, the figures we encountered left lingering questions in our minds. Were they manifestations of our fears and hopes, urging us to confront our innermost truths? Or were they messengers from a realm beyond our comprehension, offering cryptic guidance towards a higher plane of existence? The enigma surrounding their presence only fueled our curiosity, driving us to seek answers amidst the shifting landscapes of this mythical realm.

The echoes of our footsteps reverberated through the corridors of time, resonating with the echoes of past and future selves intertwined. Each encounter and revelation seemed to peel back the layers of our identities, laying bare the complexities that defined us. As we navigated through the labyrinthine passages of Olympus, it became clear that our journey was about reaching a destination and unraveling our souls' intricate tapestry.

From a couple of feet behind me, I heard Dean yell, "Dragons, run." Turning around, I saw dragons and lots of them, along with what looked like barbarians. We ran and soon saw a mountain with what looked like a castle being built into it. Getting closer, we could hear a woman yelling at the Dragathas and aiming at the dragons. There were then countless armed troops surrounding us as we started to see what almost looked like canyon fire coming from the mountainside.

As we fled from the dragons and the chaos unfolding around us, we realized that our journey through Olympus was far more complex than we had anticipated. The sight of the castle embedded within the mountain sent shivers down my spine, its ominous presence looming over us like a foreboding shadow. The woman's commanding voice pierced through the chaos, directing the troops to prepare for battle against the oncoming threat. The sound of weapons being readied and the sight of Dragathas being loaded added to the tension in the air, signaling an imminent clash of forces.

As we sought refuge amid the armed troops, the canyon fire erupting from the mountainside painted a scene of impending conflict and danger. The dragons circling above seemed to be harbingers of destruction, their fiery breath lighting up the sky with a menacing glow. The barbarians accompanying them exuded a sense of primal ferocity, adding to the sense of urgency that gripped us. The unfolding events on Olympus were a stark reminder of the unpredictable nature of our journey, where every moment held the potential for both peril and revelation.

Amid the chaos and uncertainty, a glimmer of hope flickered within me, a belief that we could overcome the challenges ahead. The echoes of the figures we had encountered resonated in my mind, reminding me of the inner strength and resilience needed to navigate the trials of Olympus. As we braced ourselves for the impending battle, I knew that our journey was not just about physical survival but about confronting the inner demons and fears that threatened to consume us. The path ahead was fraught with danger, but it also offered the promise of growth and transformation, a chance to emerge stronger and wiser from the crucible of Olympus. The clash of forces on Olympus was a testament to the fragile balance between chaos and order that governed our journey. As the dragons unleashed fiery wrath upon the canyon, the fabric of reality seemed to tremble under the weight of impending conflict. The castle's dark silhouette against the mountain was a stark reminder of the ancient powers that resided within these hallowed grounds, watching our every move with curiosity and malice. Amid the chaos, a sense of camaraderie emerged among our group, a bond forged in the crucible of adversity that strengthened our resolve to face whatever challenges lay ahead.

The echoes of past battles reverberated through the air, a haunting reminder of the sacrifices made and the losses endured in the pursuit of our quest. The woman's unwavering command echoed in my mind, a beacon of guidance in the uncertainty surrounding us. As we braced ourselves for the inevitable confrontation, a sense of determination welled within me, a fierce resolve to confront the shadows that lurked within and without. The dragons' roars mingled with the clash of weapons, creating a symphony of chaos and defiance that echoed through the canyons, a testament to the indomitable spirit of those who dared to challenge the gods themselves.

In the heart of Olympus, where danger and revelation danced hand in hand, we stood united against the forces of darkness, ready to write our destiny amidst the chaos and uncertainty that enveloped us. The journey ahead was fraught with peril, but it also held the promise of transformation and rebirth, a chance to emerge from the crucible of Olympus as survivors and warriors forged in the fires of adversity. As we gazed upon the castle's forbidding walls, I knew that our test had only begun and that the trials ahead would demand more than physical strength. It would require courage of the soul and resilience of the spirit to navigate the treacherous path ahead.

Even the hand to hand battle, along with the fight against the dragons, went on for hours. Dean, being fourteen now, was rallying with the side of good. He still knew how to use his sword against all the barbarians and their swords. A very strangely dressed woman soon joined him. She wore a blue and gold cape with a hood, gold with blue trimmed gloves, and brown knee high boots. She wielded her sword with style as she made offensive and defensive moves. She was jumping in the air while swinging her sword.

The strangely dressed woman's arrival brought a new energy to the battle. Her graceful yet powerful movements matched Dean's skill with the sword. Together, they formed a formidable team against the barbarians and dragons. The woman's blue and gold cape fluttered in the wind as she executed precise offensive and defensive maneuvers, complementing Dean's tactics seamlessly. Despite the odds stacked against them, their determination and courage never wavered.

As the battle raged on, more allies joined their cause, each bringing their unique strengths to the fight. The clash of swords, the roar of dragons, and the shouts of warriors filled the air, creating a symphony of chaos and bravery. Dean and the mysterious woman led the charge, inspiring others to stand tall and fight for what they believed in.

With every swing of the sword and every spell cast, the tide of the battle began to turn in favor of the side of good. The barbarians and dragons, once seemingly unbeatable, now faced a united front of courageous warriors determined to protect their land and loved ones. Victory was within reach, fueled by the unwavering spirit of those who fought with honor and courage. The sun began to set on the battlefield, casting a golden hue over the weary but triumphant warriors. Dean and the mysterious woman stood side by side, their breaths heavy but their spirits high. The once chaotic symphony of battle now transformed into a chorus of victory chants and cheers as the last barbarians and dragons retreated in defeat.

As the dust settled, the allies gathered around Dean and the woman, their eyes reflecting admiration and gratitude. Each warrior, with scars of battle and hearts of courage, shared a bond forged in the heat of conflict. They knew this victory was about defeating the enemy and stand-ing together in unity and strength.

Amid the celebrations, the woman removed her hood, revealing a face of wisdom and kindness that spoke of untold stories and experiences. Dean looked at her with newfound respect, rec-ognizing her as a warrior and a leader who in-spired hope and courage in others. Together, they symbolized the power of resilience and ca-maraderie in the face of adversity.

As night descended and the stars twinkled above, the warriors gathered around a crackling fire, sharing tales of bravery and camaraderie. Dean and the woman sat at the center, their presence a beacon of hope and unity. The battle may have been won, but their journey was far from over, bound by a shared purpose to protect their land and uphold the values of honor and justice. As the fire crackled and the night grew more profound, the conversation among the warriors shifted to reflections on the battles they had fought and the challenges that lay ahead. Stories of sacrifice and bravery intertwined with laughter and camaraderie, creating a tapestry of shared experiences that bound them together in a bond stronger than steel.

Dean and the woman, now known as Yawkan, Leader of the Tuathains, shared tales of their past adventures and the lessons they had learned along the way. Each word spoken carried the weight of wisdom and resilience, inspiring those around them to embrace their journeys with courage and determination. The firelight danced in their eyes, reflecting the flickering flames of passion and purpose that burned within their hearts.

As the night wore on, the warriors settled into a comfortable silence, each lost in their thoughts and memories. The stars above shone slightly brighter, casting a gentle glow over the group gathered around the fire. In that moment of quiet reflection, they found solace in knowing that no matter what trials awaited them, they would face them together, united in their commitment to protect their land and uphold the values of honor and justice.

The crackling of the fire provided a soothing soundtrack to their thoughts, a reminder of the

warmth and camaraderie that bound them together. As the embers danced in the night sky,
the warriors felt a deep sense of connection not
only to each other but also to the land they
swore to protect. Each flickering flame seemed
to whisper tales of battles won and lost, of sacrifices made in the name of a more significant
cause. In that shared moment of contemplation,
they renewed their vow to stand firm in the face
of adversity, drawing strength from the legacy of
those who came before them.

As the night deepened and the warriors basked
in the warmth of the crackling fire, a sense of
camaraderie enveloped them like a comforting
cloak. Each shared glance and nod spoke volumes of the unspoken bond that united them in
their quest for justice and protection. The flickering flames seemed to dance in rhythm with
their beating hearts, echoing the resilience and
determination that burned within each warrior's
soul.

Amid the tranquility of the night, tales of courage
and sacrifice continued to weave a tapestry of
shared experiences, binding the warriors to-

gether for a common purpose. Memories of battles won and lost mingled with laughter and solemn reflections, creating a mosaic of courage and unity that defined their journey. Dean and Yawkan, now revered as a beacon of leadership and inspiration, shared anecdotes of their past adventures, imparting valuable lessons of wisdom and fortitude to their comrades.

As the fire crackled with renewed vigor, casting long shadows that danced across the faces of the warriors, a sense of gratitude and reverence filled the air. Each warrior, marked by scars of battle and hearts of courage, found solace in the company of kindred spirits who understood the weight of their shared burdens and triumphs. The night sky above twinkled with a promise of new beginnings and uncharted paths, reminding them that their journey was far from over.

In the night's stillness, as whispers of the wind intertwined with the crackling fire, a sense of peace settled over the warriors. They knew that the road ahead would be fraught with challenges and uncertainties. Still, they also knew that, bound by a common purpose and unwavering resolve, they could overcome any obstacle that dared to take their way together. And so, under the watchful gaze of the stars and the flickering flames, they reaffirmed their commitment to stand as one, united in their quest for justice, honor, and the protection of all they held dear.

With the castle still partly unfinished, we were able to sleep in somewhat finished rooms. My mom, Dean, and I stayed in the same room, with a fabulous stone fireplace, a shelf above it, and a vast bed. I want to give you more details about the room's appearance since it was weird. There were framed baby pictures of Yawkan with a young baby boy and two three older children. There was an age difference of about ten years between the baby and the other three children.

The room exuded a sense of history and mystery, with its ancient stone fireplace and the intriguing framed baby pictures adorning the walls. As we settled in for the night, the crackling fire cast dancing shadows across the room, creating a cozy ambiance that felt almost surreal. The juxtaposition of the baby pictures with the older children hinted at a story waiting to be unraveled, a tale of family secrets and hidden connections that added an air of intrigue to our stay in the castle.

The following day, as sunlight filtered through the dusty windows, we embarked on a journey to explore more of the unfinished castle. The corridors echoed with whispers of the past, and each room held its own secrets waiting to be discovered. From hidden passages to forgotten chambers, every corner of the castle seemed to have a piece of history waiting to be uncovered. As we delved deeper into the maze-like structure, we couldn't help but wonder about the lives of those who had once walked these halls and the stories woven into the castle's very stones.

The castle's library, towering shelves of dusty books and antique manuscripts, beckoned to us with promises of forgotten knowledge and untold stories. As we ran our fingers over the spines of ancient tomes, the scent of parchment and ink filled the air, transporting us to a different era where words held the power to shape destinies and unlock mysteries.

Venturing into the castle's gardens, we were greeted by a labyrinth of overgrown hedges and statues weathered by time. Each statue seemed to guard a secret, their stoic expressions hinting at tales of love, betrayal, and loss. The winding paths led us through a maze of floral scents and hidden nooks, where we could almost hear the echoes of laughter and whispered conversations from centuries past.

As night fell once again, we found ourselves drawn to the castle's grand ballroom, its once opulent chandeliers now dimmed with age. The polished marble floors reflected the flickering candlelight, casting a soft glow over the room. We could almost envision the elegant dances and extravagant soirees that had once filled the space, the music of violins and laughter lingering in the air like a ghostly echo of the past.

That's when Yawkan, the great early Tuathain leader, walked in with Marlanaveth and three children looking to be in their teenage years. My mother looked at me, and we both looked back at the three teenagers. There was a baby boy, one boy, and two girls, and the baby looked familiar. He looked like my grandfather, the Leader of the Peace Givers from planet Celestra. With all of our thinking going on in our heads, Marlanaveth started her musical chanting again. I guess this would have been the first time for her since she's not met us yet. A little dancing accompanied her musical chanting on her part. Wow, did she have the rhythmic moves going on? This went on for about thirty minutes or so. We could see stones stacked on other rocks, and inside, the ballroom started to become once again like it had just been built, and the lights turned on. When it was all done, Yawkan walked over to us with the teenagers and baby. She introduced them to us by name; the baby was my grandfather.

That moment in the castle's grand ballroom marked the beginning of a transformation that none of us could have anticipated. As Yawkan, the great early Tuathain leader, stood before us with Marlanaveth and the three teenagers, a sense of mystery and wonder enveloped the room. The flickering candlelight seemed to dance in rhythm with Marlanaveth's enchanting musical chanting, creating an atmosphere of magic and intrigue.

As the stones stacked upon each other and the ballroom regained its former glory, a sense of nostalgia mixed with anticipation filled the air. The revelation that the baby among the teenagers was none other than the reincarnation of my grandfather, the Leader of the Peace Givers from planet Celestra, left us all in awe.

With the past and present intricately intertwined in this extraordinary moment, we couldn't help but wonder about the future that lay ahead. What other secrets and connections would be unveiled in this mystical encounter? Only time would tell as we embarked on a journey that transcended time and space, guided by the echoes of history and the promise of destiny. The echoes of history reverberated through the castle's grand ballroom, carrying a profound significance. As the mystical encounter unfolded before us, the threads of destiny intertwined with the tapestry of time, weaving a narrative that transcended mere mortal understanding. The revelation of the teenager's true identity as the reincarnation of a revered leader from a distant planet added another layer of complexity to the unfolding saga.

Amid the flickering candlelight and Marlanaveth's haunting melodies, a palpable sense of anticipation hung in the air, mingling with a deep-rooted nostalgia for a long-forgotten past. The enigmatic connection between past and present, between the known and the unknown, left us all spellbound, yearning to unravel the secrets that lay hidden within the castle's walls.

As we stood on the threshold of this extraordinary journey, guided by the whispers of fate and the echoes of generations past, we could not help but feel a sense of trepidation and exhilaration. What other mysteries awaited us in the depths of the castle's secrets? What revelations would shape our destinies and redefine our understanding of the world around us? Only time would reveal the answers as we embarked on a quest that would test the limits of our courage and the depths of our convictions. The castle's ancient walls whispered tales of forgotten legends and untold mysteries, beckoning us to delve deeper into the enigmatic past that lay shrouded in shadows. As we ventured further into the labyrinthine corridors, the echoes of history grew louder, resonating with the weight of centuries-old secrets waiting to be unveiled.

In the dimly lit chambers adorned with relics of a bygone era, we discovered cryptic symbols etched into the stone walls, hinting at a hidden language that spoke of prophecies yet to be fulfilled. The air was heavy with anticipation, charged with the energy of those who had walked these halls long before us, their presence lingering like a ghostly echo in the stillness of the night.

Each step we took brought us closer to the heart of the castle, where the convergence of past and present blurred the boundaries of reality, opening a gateway to realms beyond our wildest imagination. The fabric of time seemed to ripple and warp around us, drawing us into a web of fate and destiny that bound us to the castle's ancient legacy.

As we stood at the crossroads of history and myth, on the brink of a revelation that would shape the course of our lives forever, we knew that the journey ahead would test not only our resolve but also our understanding of the forces that guided us. The echoes of the past whispered of trials yet to come, of challenges that would push us to our limits and redefine our very existence. And so, with hearts full of courage and minds open to the unknown, we embarked on a quest that would lead us to the very edge of possibility, where the mysteries of the castle's secrets awaited their final unveiling. In the heart of the castle, a forgotten chamber beckoned to us, its ancient door creaking open to reveal a room frozen in time. Dust motes danced in the dim light, casting eerie shadows on the walls adorned with faded tapestries depicting scenes of long-forgotten battles and triumphs. The air was thick with the scent of age, a musty fragrance that spoke of centuries of neglect and solitude.

As we ventured further into the chamber, our footsteps echoing off the stone floor, we stumbled upon a crumbling pedestal upon which rested a weathered tome bound in cracked leather. Its pages whispered of lost knowledge and forbidden magic, tantalizing us with promises of power and peril. Symbols of arcane wisdom adorned the margins, their meaning shrouded in mystery and intrigue.

With trembling hands, we dared to open the tome, unleashing a surge of energy that pulsed through the chamber, illuminating the darkness with an otherworldly glow. Words written in a language long forgotten danced before our eyes, weaving a tale of ancient sorcery and untold wonders. The very fabric of reality seemed to tremble at the revelations contained within, hinting at a power beyond comprehension.

As we delved deeper into the tome's secrets, each page revealed a new layer of the castle's enigmatic past, connecting us to a lineage of seekers and guardians who had come before. The echoes of their presence reverberated through the chamber, guiding us on a journey of discovery and transformation. And so, with hearts ablaze with curiosity and minds hungry for knowledge, we embraced the mysteries that awaited us, ready to unlock the secrets of the castle's hidden legacy. As we pored over the ancient tome, each word seemed to resonate with a power beyond our understanding, drawing us deeper into the mysteries that lay hidden within the castle's walls. The pages revealed intricate spells and incantations, their cryptic symbols hinting at magic long forgotten by the world. We traced our fingers over the faded text, feeling the pulse of ancient energies thrumming beneath the surface, waiting to be unleashed.

Lost in the labyrinthine corridors of knowledge, we uncovered tales of legendary artifacts and mythical creatures that once roamed the lands surrounding the castle. Whispers of a bygone era filled the chamber, painting vivid images of heroes and villains locked in eternal struggle. The boundaries between reality and fantasy blurred as we immersed ourselves in the rich tapestry of history woven within the tome's pages.

With each revelation, reverence and awe washed over us as if we were mere mortals glimpsing the workings of gods. The weight of centuries pressed down upon us, a reminder of the responsibility of wielding such ancient power. Yet, despite the dangers lurking in the shadows, we were drawn inexorably forward, driven by a thirst for knowledge and a hunger for the truth buried in the depths of the castle's secrets.

And so, as we embarked on this journey of discovery, we knew that our lives would be forever changed by the revelations that awaited us. The legacy of the castle beckoned us to unlock its hidden truths, to unravel the mysteries that had long eluded the grasp of mortal minds. And with each step we took, we embraced the unknown with open hearts and minds, ready to confront whatever challenges lay ahead in our quest for enlightenment. As we delved deeper into the secrets of the ancient tome, the lines between reality and myth continued to blur, revealing a tapestry of stories that transcended time. Each page unveiled a new layer of history, weaving a narrative of forgotten civilizations and legendary beings that once walked the earth. The words seemed to hum with a resonance echoing through the chambers, stirring a sense of wonder and curiosity.

Amidst the tales of magic and heroism, we stumbled upon prophecies that foretold a great reckoning, a cataclysmic event that would shape the world's fate. The weight of these revelations hung heavy in the air, casting a shadow of uncertainty over our quest for knowledge. Yet, the allure of uncovering the truth behind these ancient enigmas spurred us onward, driving us to seek answers where others had faltered.

As we ventured further into the labyrinth of mysteries, we encountered challenges that tested our intellect and courage. The whispers of the past seemed to guide our steps, leading us toward a destiny intertwined with the very fabric of existence. With each riddle solved and each secret unveiled, we felt a sense of connection to a realm beyond our own, a realm where magic and reality danced in a delicate balance.

And so, with hearts ablaze with curiosity and minds sharpened by the pursuit of knowledge, we continued our journey through the annals of time, determined to uncover the truths that lay hidden within the depths of the castle's ancient texts. The legacy of those who came before us beckoned us forward, urging us to embrace the unknown and unlock the mysteries that had long eluded mortal comprehension. And as we stood on the precipice of discovery, we knew that our lives would forever be intertwined with the echoes of the past, guiding us towards a future shaped by the wisdom of ages long gone. As we unraveled the ancient tome's intricate tapestry of stories, a sense of awe and reverence enveloped us, drawing us deeper into the realm of forgotten civilizations and mythical beings. The prophecies we unearthed painted a vivid picture of a world on the brink of transformation, where the threads of fate intertwined with the echoes of the past. Each challenge we faced along our journey was a testament to our resilience and determination, forging a bond between us and the enigmatic forces that guided our path.

Amidst the labyrinth of mysteries and revelations, we found ourselves on the threshold of a revelation transcending mere knowledge, hinting at the interconnectedness of all things and weaving a web of destiny that spanned epochs. The whispers of ancient wisdom whispered secrets of a reality beyond our comprehension, beckoning us to delve deeper into the depths of the castle's archives in search of enlightenment.

With every page turned and every enigma unraveled, the veil between the mundane and the
magical grew thinner, blurring the boundaries
of what we once deemed possible. Our quest
for truth had become a pilgrimage of the soul, a
journey that transcended time and space, leading us toward a profound understanding of the
universe's intricate design. As we stood on the
threshold of a new chapter in our exploration,
we embraced the unknown with open hearts
and minds, ready to embrace the mysteries that
awaited us in the shadows of antiquity. As we
delved deeper into the ancient tome's pages, the
words seemed to come alive, resonating with a
wisdom that transcended time. The tales of forgotten civilizations and mythical beings wove a
tapestry of wonder and mystery, beckoning us to
explore realms beyond our wildest imagination.
Each prophecy uncovered added a new layer to
the intricate web of fate, revealing glimpses of a
future intertwined with the echoes of the past.

In the midst of our quest for knowledge, we
stumbled upon a revelation that surpassed
mere understanding. This revelation hinted at
the unity of all existence, where every action re-

verberated across the cosmic tapestry of reality. The whispers of ancient sages echoed through the corridors of time, guiding us toward a deeper understanding of the universe's grand design and urging us to seek enlightenment in the shadows of antiquity.

With each riddle solved and each mystery unveiled, the boundaries between the ordinary and the extraordinary blurred, opening our minds to infinite possibilities. Our journey became a pilgrimage of the soul, a sacred odyssey through the annals of history and myth, leading us towards a profound connection with the cosmic forces that shaped our destiny. As we prepared to embark on the next chapter of our adventure, we embraced the unknown with a sense of wonder and anticipation, ready to uncover the secrets hidden in the heart of the ancient tome. In the wake of our profound discoveries within the ancient tome, a sense of awe and reverence enveloped our every thought. The revelations we unearthed transcended the boundaries of conventional knowledge, leading us down a path illuminated by the wisdom of ages long past. Each symbol, each cryptic verse, held the key to unlocking mysteries that had long eluded the grasp of mortal minds.

As we delved deeper into the labyrinthine passages of the time, we encountered visions of cosmic harmony and universal interconnections. The threads of fate weaved a tapestry of existence where every being, every atom, played a vital role in the symphony of creation. The echoes of forgotten truths whispered through the veil of time, urging us to contemplate the profound unity that bound all life in a delicate dance of cosmic proportions.

With newfound clarity and purpose, we embraced the journey ahead as a sacred pilgrimage towards enlightenment. The shadows of antiquity beckoned us further, promising revelations that reshape our understanding of reality. As we stood on the unknown threshold, we felt a sense of anticipation and wonder, ready to embark on the next chapter of our odyssey through the annals of history and myth, guided by the eternal wisdom of the ancients. As we ventured deeper into the enigmatic realms of knowledge and ancient wisdom, a profound sense of interconnections permeated us. The revelations we uncovered in the sacred tome echoed through the corridors of our minds, resonating with the eternal truths that underlie the fabric of existence. Each symbol, each enigmatic verse, served as a beacon guiding us toward a deeper understanding of the cosmic tapestry that binds us all.

Amid our quest for enlightenment, we found ourselves drawn to the mysteries of the natural world, seeking to unravel the secrets that lay hidden in the whispers of the wind and the dance of the stars. The harmony of the universe unfolded before our eyes, revealing a symphony of life in which every being, every element, played a unique and irreplaceable part. The ancient wisdom we unearthed served as a bridge between the past and the present, illuminating the path toward a more profound connection with the world around us.

With hearts filled with wonder and minds open to the infinite possibilities of existence, we embarked on a new chapter of our journey, guided by the timeless wisdom of the ancients. The echoes of forgotten truths continued reverberating through our souls, urging us to delve deeper into the mysteries of the cosmos and embrace the interconnections of all things. As we set forth into the unknown, we carried with us the light of knowledge and the promise of transformation, ready to explore the boundless depths of the universe with reverence and awe. The mysteries of the cosmos beckoned us with an irresistible allure, drawing us into a realm where time seemed to lose its grip and the boundaries between the seen and the unseen blurred. As we delved deeper into the cosmic tapestry, we encountered the intricate patterns that wove together the threads of existence, revealing a grand design beyond our wildest imaginings. Each celestial body, each twinkling star, whispered ancient tales of creation and destruction, birth and rebirth, echoing the eternal dance of the universe.

In our exploration of the cosmic wonders, we came to understand that we are but fleeting specks in the vast expanse of space and time, interconnected with all that surrounds us in ways both seen and unseen. The symphony of the cosmos played on, its melodies resonating with the beating of our hearts and the thoughts that danced through our minds. We realized that in embracing the interconnections of all things, we could find solace in the knowledge that we are never truly alone in this vast and mysterious universe.

With a newfound sense of humility and awe, we continued our journey into the unknown, guided by the whispers of the ancients and the light of knowledge that illuminated our path. As we gazed upon the infinite expanse of the night sky, we felt a sense of peace wash over us, knowing that we were but a small part of a grand and magnificent whole. And so, we ventured forth with open hearts and minds, ready to embrace the mysteries that awaited us in the boundless depths of the cosmos.

5

Time Travel Laws

YAWKAN INQUIRED ABOUT ZAVEITTH'S origins and background to uncover the mystery surrounding her identity. Yawkan, unfazed by the probing question, smiled knowingly. It was as if she had anticipated this line of questioning, her demeanor calm and collected. Perhaps there was a hidden depth to Yawkan that others had yet to uncover.

As the conversation unfolded, Zaveitth's enigmatic aura grew more robust. She shared snippets of her past, each story more intriguing than the last. She hailed from a place shrouded in mystery and magic, where time seemed to move differently and legends came to life. Yawkan's eyes sparkled with ancient wisdom, hinting at a past filled with adventures and secrets.

Despite Yawkan's persistence, Zaveitth remained elusive, her past a tapestry of enigmas awaiting unraveling. It was almost as if she was a character from a tale, walking among mortals with grace and poise that spoke of a deeper connection to the world around her. The mystery of Zaveitth only deepened with each passing moment, leaving those around her captivated by her elusive charm.

Ultimately, the question of who Zaveitth was remained unanswered, lost in the mists of time and memory. But one thing was sure - Yawkan's presence was a reminder that some stories are meant to remain untold, their magic preserved in the whispers of the wind and the shadows of the night. And as Yawkan pondered the enigma that was Zaveitth, a sense of wonder and curiosity lingered, a testament to the enduring allure of the unknown.

As the whispers of Zaveitth's mysterious past faded into the night, Yawkan couldn't shake off the feeling that there was more to her story than met the eye. The enigmatic aura surrounding Zaveitth seemed to linger in the air, leaving a trail of unanswered questions. Yawkan's curiosity only deepened, fueling a desire to unravel the hidden secrets beneath the surface. It was as if Zaveitth was a puzzle waiting to be solved, a riddle that teased the mind with its complexity and depth.

With each passing day, Yawkan was drawn further into the intrigue surrounding Zaveitth. Every encounter with her revealed a new layer of mystery, a new clue that hinted at a past steeped in magic and wonder. It was clear that Zaveitth was not just a mere Tuathain; she was a being touched by something otherworldly, a creature of myths and legends brought to life in the modern world.

As Yawkan delved deeper into the enigma that was Zaveitth, she realized that some stories were not meant to be fully understood. Some mysteries were meant to remain unsolved, their allure preserved in the unknown. And as Yawkan continued her quest to unravel the secrets of Zaveitth, she understood that sometimes, the journey itself was more important than the destination. In the end, perhaps the true magic lay not in uncovering the truth but in embracing the wonder of the unknown.

As the moon rose high in the night sky, casting its ethereal glow over the land, Yawkan lost herself contemplating Zaveitth's mysterious presence. The enigmatic aura surrounding Zaveitth seemed to weave a spell of intrigue, drawing Yawkan further into the labyrinth of unanswered questions. Each encounter with Zaveitth unveiled a new facet of her enigmatic nature, leaving Yawkan with both fascination and trepidation.

It was as if Zaveitth existed on the border between reality and myth, her very being a testament to the blurred lines between the known and the unknown. Yawkan couldn't help but wonder if Zaveitth's origins were intertwined with ancient prophecies or forgotten legends, her presence a harbinger of a greater destiny yet to unfold. The whispers of the wind carried tales of Zaveitth's past, stories of magic and mystery that seemed to transcend time.

As Yawkan delved deeper into the enigma that was Zaveitth, she realized that some secrets were meant to be safeguarded, their magic preserved in the tapestries of history. The more

Yawkan sought to unravel Zaveitth's mysteries, the more she understood that some truths were better left veiled in shadows, their allure undiminished by the passage of time. And so, Yawkan embraced the enigma of Zaveitth with a sense of reverence, knowing that some stories were meant to be whispered in hushed tones, their power resonating through the ages.

While Zaveitth and I stayed up late into the early morning hours of the following day, engrossed in conversation, she revealed to me a profound secret: the baby boy we had seen earlier was, in fact, my grandfather. The realization of this familial connection between us left me in awe, envisioning the day they would finally meet, embracing the blessings of their intertwined destinies. With this newfound knowledge weighing heavily on my mind, Zaveitth entrusted me with a solemn duty to guard this secret with the utmost care, never to divulge it to another soul, whether living or deceased, for the entirety of my existence. Someone else could overhear it and make it so it won't happen if I tell anyone. So now I trust you not to tell anyone.

Furthermore, she imparted another astonishing revelation to me: our kind age at a significantly slower pace than mere mortals, underscoring the mystical essence of our lineage. Seeking solace from the weight of our conversation, we sought refuge in a cozy corner of the castle, furnished with plush chairs that cradled us in comfort. It was there, amid the tranquility of our surroundings, that Zaveitth's keen eyes detected the presence of the elusive watchers, ethereal beings cloaked in blue, yellow, and white hues, silently observing our every move.

These watchers, unseen by ordinary eyes, meticulously record our interactions, delivering their reports to the leader, who meticulously archives them for future reference. Zaveitth's keen perception allowed her to glimpse their subtle presence, shedding light on the intricate workings of our realm. As we sat enveloped in the serenity of our sanctuary, I couldn't help but ponder the enigmatic nature of our existence, intertwined with secrets and mysteries that transcended the boundaries of time itself.

It was in that particular corner where Zaveitth, in collaboration with Yawkan, who up until that moment had been entirely unfamiliar with the concept of time travel, embarked on a journey of discovery. With meticulous attention and profound contemplation, these two individuals delved into the intricate realm of time travel, ultimately crafting the fundamental laws that govern this enigmatic phenomenon. As they delved deeper into the complexities of temporal manipulation, they encountered various challenges and anomalies that tested the very fabric of their understanding.

For instance, they pondered the implications of altering past events and their potential repercussions on the present and future. Through extensive discussions and theoretical debates, Zaveitth and Yawkan explored the intricacies of paradoxes and causality loops, seeking to establish a coherent framework that could withstand the test of time itself. Their collaboration was not merely a scholarly pursuit but a profound exploration of the boundaries of reality and the essence of existence.

Furthermore, as they drafted the black and white laws of time travel, they drew inspiration from historical accounts and fictional narratives depicting temporal interference's consequences. By examining these diverse sources, they gained valuable insights into the ethical dilemmas and philosophical problems inherent in manipulating the flow of time. Their work was a theoretical exercise and a moral imperative to safeguard the temporal continuum's integrity and preserve the universe's delicate balance.

In conclusion, the partnership between Zaveitth and Yawkan symbolized a harmonious blend of knowledge and creativity as they ventured into uncharted territories of time and space. Their collaborative efforts culminated in creating a foundational framework that would guide future generations of time travelers, ensuring that the mysteries of temporal dynamics were approached with reverence and wisdom. This corner, once a mere physical location, now stood as a testament to the intellectual prowess and visionary insight of two extraordinary minds united in a quest for temporal enlightenment.

Time travel, a concept that has intrigued human-ity for centuries, is now governed by strict laws that leave no room for ambiguity. These laws, meticulously crafted and universally accepted, serve as the guiding principles for all beings ven-turing into the realm of temporal manipulation.

Imagine an individual traveling back in time to alter a significant historical event. According to these laws, such an act is strictly prohibited as it could have unforeseen consequences on the fabric of reality. This prohibition maintains the timeline's integrity and prevents any disruptions that could lead to catastrophic outcomes.

Furthermore, the laws of time travel dictate that any changes made in the past must be done with utmost caution and consideration for potential ripple effects. For instance, if a traveler were to prevent a natural disaster from occurring in the past, they must be prepared to deal with the repercussions that may arise in the present or future due to their actions.

In essence, these laws safeguard against reck-less manipulation of the temporal continuum, ensuring that time travel is used responsibly and ethically. By adhering to these regulations, beings from all corners of the universe can engage in temporal journeys, knowing that they are upholding the fundamental principles of time travel governance.

Law of Non-Interference

- It is strictly forbidden to alter the course of events in the past that could potentially impact the future timeline.

Law of Temporal Anchors

- All time travelers must have a designated temporal anchor to ensure a safe return to their original timeline.

Law of Preservation

- Historical artifacts and events must be preserved in their original state to maintain the integrity of the timeline.

Law of Paradoxes

- Any actions that could create paradoxes or contradictions in the timeline are prohibited.

Law of Temporal Guardians

- Time travelers must uphold their duty as guardians of time, protecting its sanctity and preventing unauthorized temporal incursions.-

Law of Time Loops

-Time loops must be carefully monitored and controlled to prevent infinite recursion and potential damage to the timeline.

Law of Alternate Realities

- Exploration of alternate realities is allowed under strict supervision to avoid cross-contamination with the primary timeline.

Law of Temporal Healing

- Time travelers are responsible for correcting temporal anomalies and restoring balance to disrupted timelines.

Law of Temporal Records

- Accurate and detailed records of all temporal journeys must be maintained for future reference and analysis.

Law of Temporal Ethics

- Time travelers must adhere to a strict code of ethics governing their interactions with past and future individuals to prevent unintended consequences.- Law of Temporal Paradoxes

- Avoid creating paradoxes by interfering with past events that could lead to contradictory outcomes.

Law of Temporal Nexus

- Recognize significant temporal nexus points and exercise caution when making decisions that could alter their course.

Law of Temporal Guardians

- Designate individuals responsible for safeguarding the integrity of the timeline and enforcing temporal laws.

Law of Temporal Research

- Conduct thorough research before planning time travel missions to minimize unforeseen consequences.

Law of Temporal Oversight

- Establish regulatory bodies to oversee and regulate time travel activities to prevent misuse and maintain temporal stability.- Law of Temporal Ethics

- Uphold ethical standards when engaging in time travel activities to ensure respect for historical events and individuals.

Law of Temporal Consequences

- Acknowledge that every action in the past can have ripple effects on the present and future, necessitating careful consideration of choices.

Law of Temporal Limitations

- Recognize the limitations of time travel technology and refrain from attempting to alter events beyond the scope of feasibility.

Law of Temporal Preservation

- Preserve the natural flow of time by refraining from unnecessary interference in historical events, allowing for the organic progression of timelines.

Law of Temporal Unity

- Strive to maintain unity across temporal realities by avoiding actions that could lead to divergent timelines and fragmentation of the time-space continuum.

I understand that processing and retaining this information might initially seem overwhelming. It's essential to remember that these laws were established to safeguard the timelines of all beings and events. Yawkan and her civilization are relatively new to the concept of time travel and have yet to unlock its secrets officially. The journey towards discovering time travel is a mysterious path, with uncertainties regarding when and how this breakthrough will occur. Moreover, the method they will use to traverse from their home planet Olympus, to the distant planet Celestra remains a puzzle, especially considering their lack of advanced space travel technologies, as observed so far. The intricacies of their eventual discovery and the challenges they may face in bridging the gap between worlds are shrouded in uncertainty and intrigue.

Now, as Yawkan and her civilization embark on the daunting journey toward unraveling the mysteries of time travel, they face not only the challenges of scientific exploration but also the ethical dilemmas that come with manipulating the fabric of time itself. The implications of altering timelines and potentially disrupting the natural order of events raise profound questions about the consequences of their actions. Will they be able to navigate the delicate balance between curiosity and responsibility as they venture into uncharted territory?

Moreover, time travel's cultural and societal impact cannot be overlooked. How will the discovery of this groundbreaking technology shape the beliefs and practices of Yawkan's civilization? Will it lead to a newfound sense of unity and understanding, or will it sow seeds of discord and division as different factions vie for control over this powerful tool?

As Yawkan and her peers grapple with the enigma of time travel, one thing remains certain: the journey ahead is fraught with uncertainty and intrigue, promising remarkable discoveries and unforeseen challenges. Only time will tell what lies in store for them as they navigate the uncharted waters of temporal exploration. Now, as Yawkan and her civilization delve deeper into the complexities of time travel, the ethical considerations become even more intricate. Altering past events or foreseeing the future raises profound moral dilemmas that challenge their core values and beliefs. How will they navigate the fine line between pursuing knowledge and preserving the natural order of time? Will they resist the temptation to meddle with history for personal gain, or will the allure of changing fate prove too strong to resist?

Furthermore, the societal implications of mastering time travel are vast and multifaceted. The newfound ability to traverse different eras could revolutionize their understanding of history, culture, and identity. Will this groundbreaking technology foster a sense of unity and cooperation among Yawkan's people, or will it sow seeds of discord and division as conflicting interests clash over the control of temporal manipulation? The potential for positive transformation and catastrophic consequences looms as they navigate the uncharted territory of temporal exploration.

As Yawkan and her companions press onward in their quest for temporal enlightenment, the unpredictable nature of their journey becomes increasingly apparent. The allure of unlocking the secrets of time itself is tempered by the realization that their actions could have far-reaching repercussions, shaping not only their destiny but also the fabric of reality itself. In this uncharted frontier of temporal discovery, every decision carries weight; every choice reverberates through the annals of time. They hope to unravel the mysteries that lie ahead only by treading carefully and thoughtfully.

We heard a loud crash and a splash from somewhere in the distance.

We heard a loud crash and a splash from somewhere in the distance. The sudden noise echoed through the stillness, sending ripples of curiosity through our minds. As we strained to discern the source of the disturbance, our senses heightened, attuned to the mysterious event unfolding beyond our immediate surroundings.

With bated breath, we scanned the horizon, searching for any visual clues that might shed light on the origin of the crash and splash. Was it a falling tree, a large wave crashing against the shore, or perhaps a playful pod of dolphins leaping out of the water? The possibilities seemed endless, each one more intriguing than the last.

As the echoes of the sound slowly faded into the distance, leaving us with only the gentle rustling of leaves and the distant hum of nature, we were left pondering the enigmatic nature of the world around us. Every sound and movement held the potential for surprise and wonder, reminding us of the vastness and complexity of our universe. With a sense of anticipation lingering in the air, we remained fixated on the unknown origin of the disruptive crash and splash. The lingering echoes of the event continued to resonate in our minds, fueling our imagination with endless possibilities. Was it a rare occurrence of nature's raw power, a hidden creature making its presence known, or simply a trick of the elements playing with our senses?

As we delved deeper into the mystery, our surroundings seemed to come alive with hidden secrets waiting to be uncovered. Every rustle of leaves and every distant call of a bird held a hint of the unknown, inviting us to explore the enigmatic depths of our surroundings. The world around us became a tapestry of intrigue, woven with threads of curiosity and wonder, waiting for us to unravel its mysteries.

In that moment of contemplation, we realized that the world's beauty lies in its visible wonders and the hidden marvels that lurk beneath the surface. The crash and splash that had initially startled us now reminded us of nature's boundless mysteries, encouraging us to embrace the unknown with open hearts and curious minds.

As we all hurriedly exited the grand entrance of the majestic castle, I couldn't resist the urge to pause and admire the breathtaking sight before me. The castle stood tall and proud, its intricate architecture a testament to the craftsmanship of its builders. With a sense of awe, I tore my gaze away and refocused on reaching the nearby body of water to investigate the loud crash that had captured our attention.

Pushing through the dense foliage, we finally emerged at the edge of Lake Wathaian, its tranquil surface now marred by a plume of dark gray smoke billowing into the sky. The scene was ominous, hinting at some unseen danger lurking ahead. Then we noticed a figure in the water, their features obscured by the distance and haze. As we drew closer, the details became more apparent: a person with dark, short hair and a strong, muscular build lay partially submerged in the water.

My mother, ever the voice of reason and compassion, knelt beside the unconscious individual. With gentle hands, she carefully turned their head to check for signs of life. The tension in the air was palpable as we waited for any indication of breathing. The stranger's fate hung in the balance, a mystery begging to be unraveled amid the chaos around us.

At that moment, the lake's stillness contrasted sharply with our actions' urgency. Every movement, every breath felt magnified in the face of the unknown. The realization dawned upon us that our journey had taken an unexpected turn, plunging us into a situation fraught with uncertainty and danger. As we stood on the brink of discovery, the echoes of the castle's ancient walls seemed to whisper secrets of the past, urging us to unravel the enigma before us. The stranger's eyelids fluttered a faint sign of life amid the stillness of the lake. My heart skipped a beat as hope mingled with apprehension. What led this mysterious individual to this isolated, unconscious, vulnerable spot? Questions swirled in my mind, adding another layer of complexity to the unfolding drama.

As my mother continued her gentle examination, a rustling in the bushes nearby caught our attention. A group of elves emerged, their faces etched with concern and curiosity. They had witnessed the commotion from afar and rushed to assist. In their eyes, I saw a reflection of our bewilderment and determination to uncover the truth behind this enigmatic scene.

Together, we carefully lifted the stranger out of the water, cradling them with care and respect. The weight of their body in our arms felt significant, a tangible reminder of the fragile balance between life and death. As we carried the unconscious figure toward the safety of the shore, a sense of camaraderie and shared purpose united us in this crisis.

The sun dipped below the horizon, casting long shadows across the lake's surface. The fading light seemed to mirror the hope that initially gripped us. Yet, a glimmer of resilience shone through as we laid the stranger down on the soft grass, determined to uncover the truth behind their mysterious appearance. As the night descended, enveloping us in its embrace, the echoes of the castle's ancient walls whispered of challenges yet to come, urging us to stand firm in the face of adversity.

Marlanaveth looked around and said she'd bring some light to the scene. With some short rhythmic Gaelic chanting, she caused firelit torches to appear high above the ground. The scene was as if it wasn't even dark. The person we had pulled into the grass was a man with a colorful inked image on his left bicep of a torn heart, one half blue, and the other half red. There was an arrow going between the two halves. The blue half had the letter P, while the red had L.

Marlanaveth's enchanting Gaelic chanting filled the air with mystical energy, illuminating the surroundings with flickering torchlight. The intricate tattoo on the mysterious man's arm captured our attention, its symbolism hinting at a deeper story waiting to be unveiled. The torn heart, divided between blue and red halves marked with the letters P and L, sparked questions in our minds. What tale did this inked design tell? Was it a clue to the man's identity or a reflection of his inner turmoil?

As we gazed at the intricate tattoo, a sense of urgency gripped us, driving our determination to unravel the enigma surrounding the unconscious stranger. With their keen eyes and ancient wisdom, the elves exchanged knowing glances, silently acknowledging the tattoo's significance. It seemed to hold the key to unlocking the mysteries hidden within the man's past, connecting us all in a shared quest for truth and understanding.

With each passing moment, the night

It enveloped us in its darkness, casting long shadows across the grassy shore. The torches flickered in the gentle breeze, casting an ethereal glow on the scene before us. The man's eyelids fluttered once more, a sign of consciousness stirring. The tension in the air was palpable as we awaited his awakening, bracing ourselves for the revelations that lay ahead.

As the last remnants of daylight faded into the night, we stood united by a common purpose to uncover the secrets buried within the depths of the man's past. The echoes of the castle's ancient walls whispered of challenges yet to come, urging us to stand resilient in the face of adversity. And as the man's eyes slowly opened, revealing a glint of recognition and determination, we knew our journey had only begun. The mysterious man's eyes slowly adjusted to the flickering torchlight, showing a depth of emotion that mirrored the intricate tattoo on his arm. A sense of determination radiated as he sat up, a silent promise of cooperation in our shared quest for truth. With their timeless wisdom, the elves approached him cautiously, their eyes reflecting a blend of curiosity and respect for the enigma he embodied.

With each passing moment, the night seemed to whisper secrets of its own, urging us to delve deeper into the mysteries surrounding us. The man's gaze met ours, silently acknowledging the bond forged between strangers united by a common purpose. His tattoo, once a symbol of mystery, now seemed to beckon us closer, inviting us to unravel the threads of his past and discover the truths hidden within.

As the torches cast long shadows across the grassy shore, we felt a renewed sense of purpose wash over us, a determination to stand firm in the face of whatever challenges lay ahead. The castle walls echoed with the weight of history, their ancient stones bearing witness to the unfolding drama. As the man spoke his first words, his voice resonated with a blend of vulnerability and resilience, marking the beginning of a journey filled with twists and revelations yet to come. The night air hung heavy with anticipation, each breath filled with the promise of revelations yet to unfold. Once shrouded in mystery, the man's presence now stood as a beacon guiding us toward the heart of the unknown. His eyes, pools of untold stories, held a depth that mirrored the ancient secrets whispered by the night itself.

As we ventured deeper into the castle's labyrinthine corridors, the echoes of history grew louder, resonating with the weight of forgotten tales waiting to be unearthed. With their timeless grace, the elves moved with a fluidity that spoke of centuries-old wisdom, their silent guidance leading us toward the truth we sought.

With each step, the man's tattoo seemed to pulse with a life of its own, a tapestry of symbols hinting at a past filled with darkness and light. The torchlight flickered, casting dancing shadows that seemed to dance to the rhythm of the unfolding narrative, a silent witness to the enigma that stood before us.

And as we stood on the precipice of discovery, a sense of unity washed over us, binding strangers together in a shared quest for understanding. The man's voice, a blend of vulnerability and strength, resonated through the ancient halls, marking the beginning of a journey that would test our courage and unravel the mysteries of the past.

He told us his name was Lucus, which carried a sense of mystery and strength. Lucus hailed from the distant planet Angleac, a world shrouded in legends and tales of bravery. Situated within the vast Celestial Spiral galaxy, Angleac sparkled like a precious gem amidst the cosmic expanse. It was a place where the skies danced with hues of purple and gold, a sight that mesmerized all who beheld it.

In his time on Angleac, Lucus had been a formidable member of an elite guard force, a group tasked with upholding peace and order across the planet. His training was rigorous, honing his skills in combat and strategy to perfection. Lucus stood as a beacon of hope for his people, symbolizing his unwavering dedication to justice.

Through countless battles and challenges, Lucus had proven himself time and time again, earning the respect and admiration of all who knew him. His leadership on the battlefield was unmatched, inspiring his comrades to fight with courage and conviction. In the face of adversity, Lucus remained steadfast, his resolve unbreakable like the mountains of Angleac.

As he shared his stories with us, his eyes sparkled with memories of triumph and sacrifice. Lucus's journey from a humble warrior to a legendary guardian was a testament to his unwavering commitment to his duty. The tales of his exploits echoed through the halls of Angleac, a reminder of the indomitable spirit within him.

In every word he spoke, Lucus embodied the essence of a true hero, a protector of peace, and a champion of justice. His presence among us was a gift, a reminder of the power of resilience and the importance of standing up for what is right. Lucus's legacy would endure for generations to come, a shining example of courage and honor in the vast tapestry of the cosmos.

6
Truth Will Be Told

H IS MYSTERIOUS PAST UNRAVELED with each passing day, revealing a web of deceit and hidden secrets. The enigmatic aura that surrounded him slowly dissipated, giving way to a tangled web of lies and deception that had been carefully woven over time. Each revelation peeled back a layer of his meticulously constructed intricate facade, exposing the dark truths that lurked beneath the surface. It was like watching a carefully crafted illusion crumble before everyone's eyes, leaving a sense of disbelief and betrayal behind.

People who once trusted him now questioned every word that came out of his mouth, unsure what else he might be hiding. Those who had placed their faith in him were grappling with doubt and uncertainty, reevaluating every interaction and conversation they had shared. The once unwavering trust had now been replaced by a lingering sense of suspicion, casting a shadow of doubt over every promise and assurance he made. It was a stark reminder of how easily perception could be manipulated, and trust could be shattered.

The once charming facade crumbled, exposing the darkness that lurked beneath the surface. What was once perceived as charisma and charm now revealed itself as a carefully crafted mask to conceal the shadows that dwelled within. The smiles that once lit up the room now seemed hollow and insincere, a stark juxtaposition to the sinister motives hidden behind the facade. It was a sobering realization of how appearances could be deceiving and how easily one could be misled by surface level charm.

As the truth emerged, relationships shattered, leaving behind a trail of betrayal and heartache. The unfolded revelations tore through the fabric of trust that had bound relationships together, leaving behind a wake of broken promises and shattered illusions. Friendships that once stood firm now crumbled under the weight of deception, leaving a sense of betrayal and heartache long after the truth had been exposed. It was a painful reminder of how fragile relationships could be when built on a foundation of lies and deceit.

What seemed like a simple facade turned out to be a complex tapestry of lies and manipulation, leaving everyone stunned by the depth of deception. The intricate layers of falsehoods carefully woven together revealed a level of cunning and manipulation that left everyone in disbelief. What appeared on the surface as a straightforward facade was a labyrinth of deceit and treachery, betrayals deceived, questioning their judgment. It was a sobering lesson in the art of deception and a stark reminder of how easily a well crafted facade could mislead one.

This man we once had trusted turned out to be the founder of an unpeaceful empire. It was shocking to discover that the very individual we trusted was behind establishing a dominion characterized by disharmony and discord. The ripple effects of this revelation were profound, casting a shadow of doubt over our previous perceptions.

An elf from the planet of Lucus informed us that this empire was the Lucusion Empire. The disclosure came from an unexpected source, an elf hailing from the same planet as the empire, Lucus. This revelation added a layer of complexity to the situation, as it was an outsider who shed light on the true nature of the empire. The elf's insight served as a wake-up call, prompting us to reevaluate our understanding of the Lucusion Empire.

They fed off lies, deceit, and anything else unkind. These are the foundations upon which the Lucusion Empire was built, a bedrock of falsehoods, deception, and cruelty. It thrived on a diet of untruths and malicious intent, perpetuating a cycle of mistrust and hatred among its inhabitants. The insidious nature of the empire's practices painted a grim picture of a society fueled by negativity and manipulation.

The leader of the peaceful beings on that planet doesn't use force but lets all beings have their own choices about what they will do. In stark contrast to the oppressive regime of the Lucusion Empire, the leader of the peaceful beings on

Lucus adopted a philosophy rooted in non-co-ercion. Rather than imposing their will through force, this leader embraced a philosophy of autonomy and free will, allowing all beings on the planet to make their own choices and chart their paths. This approach fostered a sense of empowerment and respect among the inhabitants, creating a harmonious environment based on mutual understanding and acceptance.

The Lucusion Empire's downfall was inevitable, as any society founded on deceit and oppression is bound to crumble under the weight of its falsehoods. The very fabric of the empire was woven with threads of manipulation and hostility, leading to a toxic environment where trust was a rare commodity and fear reigned supreme. The revelation of the empire's true nature catalyzed change, sparking a movement among the inhabitants to break free from the chains of tyranny and reclaim their autonomy.

As the peaceful beings on Angleac stood in stark contrast to the Lucusion Empire, their leader's philosophy of non-coercion and respect for individual choice resonated deeply with the disillusioned citizens. The leader's approach of empowering each being to make their own decisions paved the way for a new era of harmony and cooperation on the planet. Through mutual understanding and acceptance, the inhabitants of Angleac embarked on a journey towards rebuilding their society based on principles of compassion and unity.

The aftermath of the empire's collapse was marked by a period of introspection and reconciliation as the former subjects of the Lucusion Empire grappled with the scars left by years of oppression. However, guided by the example set forth by the peaceful beings and their leader, the inhabitants of Angleac began the process of healing and rebuilding. Together, they forged a very new path forward, one that embraced diversity, empathy, and the fundamental right of every being to live freely and authentically.

The legacy of the Lucusion Empire served as a cautionary tale, a reminder of the dangers of unchecked power and the importance of upholding values of integrity and compassion. Through their collective efforts, the inhabitants of Angleac transformed their planet into a beacon of hope and resilience, a testament to the enduring power of unity and cooperation. As they looked towards the future, they did so with a renewed sense of purpose and a commitment to never again allow darkness to overshadow the light of their shared humanity.

The emergence of a new governing system on Angleac, rooted in principles of transparency and accountability, ushered in an era of unprecedented growth and prosperity for the planet. The leaders of the reformed society understood the importance of fostering an environment where every voice was heard, every perspective valued, and every decision made with the collective good in mind. Through open dialogue and collaboration, they laid the foundation for a truly inclusive and equitable society where diversity was celebrated as a strength rather than a source of division.

Education became a cornerstone of the new Angleac society, focusing on nurturing critical thinking, empathy, and a deep appreciation for the interconnections of all beings. The schools were all transformed into centers of learning and exploration, where individuals of all ages were encouraged to question, innovate, and contribute to the community's collective wisdom by investing in its inhabitants' intellectual and emotional development. The Anglican government ensured a bright and sustainable future for generations to come.

The renaissance of Angleac extended beyond its borders, inspiring neighboring planets to reevaluate their own governance structures and societal norms. The success story of Angleac served as a beacon of hope for those struggling under oppressive regimes, offering a blueprint for peaceful revolution and transformative change. Through cultural exchanges and diplomatic initiatives, Angleac forged alliances based on mutual respect and shared values, fostering a network of interconnected worlds committed to upholding justice, equality, and the universal rights of all sentient beings.

As the echoes of the Lucusion Empire's downfall faded into history, a new chapter unfolded for the inhabitants of Angleac and beyond. United by a shared vision of a harmonious and just universe, they embarked on a collective journey towards a future defined not by past mistakes but by the boundless potential of a united galaxy working together for the betterment of all. In this new era of cooperation and understanding, the lessons learned from the rise and fall of the Lucusion Empire served as a guiding light, illuminating the path toward a brighter tomorrow for all who called the cosmos their home.

Now, the question arises as to what actions should be taken with Lucus, a character who was not welcomed even on his planet. The decision ultimately fell into the hands of Yawkan and Zaveitth. Together, they deliberated and concluded that Lucus's knowledge could be invaluable in training the new knights of peace, who would later be known as the Magnusteers. An alternative fate awaited Lucus, being left to the mercy of the lake. However, it was clear that the former option was more favorable. Hence, the choice was made to integrate Lucus into the Tuathain army precisely to mold the first cohort of Magnusteers.

In the realm of training, Lucus imparted essential skills to the Magnusteers. For instance, he demonstrated the art of wielding a thin sword with a protective hilt, known as a rapier, ensuring the safety of the wielder's hand. Offensive tactics like lunging, feinting, and remising were among the techniques Lucus shared with the eager trainees. Moreover, he emphasized the importance of defensive maneuvers such as riposting, parrying, and stepping. In addition, Lucus introduced various stances like the ox ward, plow ward, and fool ward to enhance the Magnusteers' combat prowess.

As the training progressed, some of the Magnusteers displayed a heightened enthusiasm, perhaps getting carried away in the heat of the moment. Recognizing the need for a respite, Lucus wisely granted them a day of rest. After all, they had been diligently learning and practicing for consecutive days, and a brief interlude would undoubtedly rejuvenate their spirits and sharpen their focus for the challenges ahead. Thus, under the leadership of Captain Elizaveth, the Magnusteers embarked on a journey of growth and mastery under Lucus's expert guidance.

Lucus proposed a daring expedition to explore uncharted territories beyond the borders of Tuathain. The idea of venturing into the unknown sparked excitement and curiosity among the Magnusteers. They eagerly prepared for the journey, gathering supplies and precisely mapping their route. As they set off into the wilderness, the lush landscapes and unfamiliar terrain presented challenges and opportunities for the team. With his navigation and survival skills expertise, Lucus led the way confidently, instilling a sense of unity and camaraderie among the group.

The Magnusteers eagerly accepted the challenge, ready to test their newfound skills in real-world scenarios. Each member brought unique abilities, whether archery, herbalism knowledge, or elemental magic proficiency. Together, they formed a formidable team, united by their shared goal of exploration and discovery. Along the way, they encountered diverse wildlife, from graceful deer to cunning wolves, providing valuable lessons in adaptation and observation. The expedition expanded their geographical knowledge and forged bonds that would last a lifetime.

During their expedition, the Magnusteers encountered mythical beasts like the majestic Griffin and the elusive Phoenix. Shrouded in mystery and legend, these creatures captivated the team with their beauty and power. Lucus, with his deep understanding of magical creatures, guided them on how to approach and interact with these beings. He emphasized the importance of respect and caution, highlighting the need to establish a mutual understanding rather than resorting to confrontation. Through careful observation and communication, the Magnusteers learned to appreciate the unique qualities of each mythical beast, gaining insight into the delicate balance between humans and magical creatures.

As they delved deeper into the heart of the unknown, the Magnusteers encountered even rarer and more enigmatic beings, such as the ethereal Sirens and the ancient Dragons. These encounters tested their courage and wit, pushing them to think creatively and act decisively in the face of danger. Lucus's guidance proved invaluable, giving them strategies to navigate these encounters gracefully and diplomatically. Each interaction with a mythical beast became a lesson in humility and empathy, reinforcing the Magnusteers' commitment to preserving the harmony between the natural and supernatural realms.

The Magnusteers encountered ancient artifacts of great power and significance deep within the mysterious forests. These relics, imbued with magic and history, whispered tales of forgotten kingdoms and lost civilizations. With his extensive knowledge of arcane symbols and ancient languages, Lucus deciphered the secrets hidden within these artifacts, unraveling their true purpose and potential. The Magnusteers marveled at the craftsmanship and ingenuity of the ancient civilizations, realizing the profound impact these artifacts could have on the present and future.

Through Lucus's guidance, the Magnusteers learned to harness the power of these ancient artifacts for the greater good. They discovered how to channel the magic within them to heal the land, protect the vulnerable, and restore balance to the natural world. Each artifact symbolized hope and renewal, a reminder of the interconnections between past and present. As they continued their exploration, the Magnusteers carried these artifacts with them, not as objects of curiosity but as tools of transformation and enlightenment. Their journey had evolved from a simple expedition into a quest for wisdom and unity, guided by the legacy of those who came before them.

I went against my mother's wishes and tagged along for the trip. Despite her initial concerns, I immersed myself in a world of learning and discovery. Throughout the journey, I absorbed valuable lessons from a myriad of sources. From the seasoned travelers we met along the way to the locals who shared their wisdom, I was like a sponge soaking up knowledge.

One of the most unexpected lessons came in the form of combat training. I never imagined myself wielding a sword, but under the guidance of a skilled instructor, I learned how to defend myself with grace and precision. The art of sword fighting honed my physical abilities and instilled a sense of discipline and focus.

As I reflect on the trip, I realize that every encounter every experience, contributed to my growth and understanding of the world. Whether navigating through bustling markets or engaging in deep conversations with new friends, each moment left an indelible mark on my journey. I emerged from the trip not only with newfound skills but also with a broader perspective on life.

Ultimately, going against my mother's wishes led me to self-discovery and enlightenment. The trip was not just a physical journey but a transformative experience that shaped my outlook on the world. I am grateful for the challenges and opportunities that came my way, as they have made me stronger, wiser, and more resilient. As I returned from the transformative journey, I carried a newfound sense of purpose and determination. The experiences I encountered along the way ignited a passion to continue seeking knowledge and growth in all aspects of my life.

One particularly impactful lesson resonated with resonated resilience's importance in facing adversity. Through the challenges I faced during the trip, whether navigating unfamiliar terrain or overcoming personal doubts, I learned the value of perseverance and inner strength. These lessons have since become guiding principles in my everyday life, pushing me to push beyond my comfort zone and embrace new opportunities with courage.

Moreover, the connections I forged with people from diverse backgrounds during the journey opened my eyes to the beauty of cultural exchange and the power of human connection. Each interaction, whether fleeting or profound, enriched my understanding of the world and reinforced the significance of empathy and compassion in bridging differences.

As I integrate the lessons learned from my journey into my daily routine, I am reminded of the profound impact that stepping outside one's comfort zone can have on personal growth and self-discovery. Embracing challenges, seeking new experiences, and remaining open to the wisdom of others are now integral parts of my journey toward self-improvement and fulfillment.

7
Every Legend There is
A Beginning

My mother, Elizaveth, emerged as a pivotal figure within the Tuathain community during our expedition, which spanned approximately three to four days. Her transformation into a respected leader, confidante, and friend has been remarkable. The villagers have come to admire and look up to her for her kind and caring nature and her exceptional ability to empathize with others and offer unwavering support in times of need.

I vividly recall a particular incident where Elizaveth went out of her way to assist a struggling community member. Not only did she provide practical help, but she also lent a compassionate ear and words of encouragement, showcasing her genuine concern for others. Actions like these have solidified her reputation as a compassionate and dedicated individual within the Tuathain society.

Elizaveth's impact extends beyond mere words; her actions speak volumes about her character and unwavering commitment to the well-being of those around her. Whether consoling a grieving friend or rallying the community in adversity, she consistently demonstrates her willingness to go above and beyond for others. Her genuine empathy and selfless deeds have earned the admiration and respect of many, who now see her as a beacon of hope and strength.

Elizaveth's journey from a regular community member to a revered leader exemplifies her exceptional qualities and steadfast dedication to serving others. As she continues embodying the virtues of kindness, empathy, and support, her community influence grows exponentially each day.

As for myself, I had never foreseen the extraordinary journey that would lead me to carve out a legendary status in the annals of time. The tales and myths that would reverberate through the corridors of history were beyond my wildest imagination. Let me take you on an exquisite, captivating journey through the realms of planets, across diverse eras, and even into different dimensions, converging into my odyssey. Let me tell you every detail, even down to the battles not fought but won with caring and understanding, even when it meant that I might die in the process.

Reflecting on my unexpected path, I recall the countless challenges I faced that shaped me into who I am today. From navigating treacherous terrains to overcoming formidable foes, each hurdle presented an opportunity for growth and self-discovery. For instance, there was a time when I found myself stranded on a distant planet, surrounded by unknown creatures and facing imminent danger. Through sheer determination and quick thinking, I survived and forged alliances that would prove invaluable in future endeavors.

Moreover, my journey transcended mere physical boundaries, delving into the depths of time itself. I witnessed the rise and fall of civilizations and the ebb and flow of power across centuries.

Exploring different eras allowed me to appreciate the nuances of each period, from the simplicity of ancient times to the complexity of modern societies. During these temporal transitions, I learned the value of adaptability and resilience, traits that would serve me well in adversity.

Venturing into alternate dimensions was perhaps the most surreal aspect of my odyssey. The laws of physics seemed to bend and warp, presenting me with challenges unlike any I had encountered before. Navigating these metaphysical realms required courage and a deep understanding of the interconnectedness of all things. In one such dimension, I encountered beings of pure energy who communicated through thoughts alone, expanding my perception of reality beyond conventional limits.

As for myself, I had never anticipated the extraordinary journey that would ultimately lead me to establish a legendary status in the annals of time. The tales and myths that would echo through the corridors of history far surpassed my wildest imagination. Allow me to guide you through a mesmerizing expedition with intri-

cate details across the realms of celestial bodies, spanning diverse eras and transcending into
alternate dimensions, all converging into my
odyssey. Let me recount every aspect, even delving into the battles not waged but triumphed
through compassion and insight, even at the risk
of hazardous, dangerous consequences.

Reflecting on my unforeseen path, I reminisce
about the challenges I encountered, molding
me into who I am today. From navigating per-
ilous terrains to vanquishing formidable adversaries, each obstacle presented an opportunity
for personal growth and self-realization. For instance, there was an occasion when I found myself stranded on a remote planet, surrounded
by enigmatic beings and facing imminent peril.
Through sheer resolve and astute decision-mak-
ing, I survived and forged alliances that would
prove invaluable in forthcoming ventures.

Furthermore, my odyssey transcended mere
physical boundaries, delving into the depths of
time itself. I bore witness to the ascendancy
and decline of civilizations, the undulating tides
of power across centuries. Exploring diverse

epochs enabled me to discern the subtleties of each era, from the simplicity of antiquity to the intricacies of contemporary societies. During these temporal transitions, I gleaned the true essence of adaptability and resilience, qualities that would stand me in good stead in times of adversity.

Venturing into alternate dimensions proved to be the most surreal facet of my odyssey. The laws of physics appeared to contort and distort, presenting challenges unlike any I had hitherto encountered. Navigating these metaphysical realms demanded courage and a profound comprehension of the interconnectedness of all existence. In one such dimension, I encountered entities of pure energy communicating through telepathy alone, expanding my perception of reality beyond conventional bounds. Continuing on this extraordinary odyssey, I delved deeper into the mysteries of the cosmos, seeking answers to existential questions that had long eluded me. Traversing through the vast expanse of space, I encountered celestial phenomena that defied conventional understanding, sparking a sense of awe and wonder. Witnessing the birth of stars and the collapse of galaxies served as a poignant reminder of the impermanence of all things, instilling a profound appreciation for the beauty and chaos inherent in the universe.

As I journeyed through the annals of time, I realized the interconnectedness of past, present, and future, each moment a thread woven into the tapestry of existence. The lessons learned from ancient civilizations resonated with me, offering insights into the cyclical nature of history and the enduring legacy of human endeavor. From the wisdom of antiquity to the innovations of tomorrow, I embraced the continuum of knowledge, recognizing that true enlightenment lies in embracing the diversity of human experience.

Venturing further into uncharted territories, I encountered beings of unfathomable wisdom and power, entities that transcended mortal comprehension. Their presence challenged my perceptions of reality, pushing the boundaries of my understanding and inviting me to question the very fabric of existence. In their ethereal presence, I found solace and enlightenment, a glimpse into the infinite possibilities beyond our limited perception's confines.

What I believe genuinely genuinelyated the start of my journey towards becoming a legendary figure was the unforgettable moment when Lucus, my beloved mother Elizaveth, and I found ourselves standing atop the majestic peak of Olympus, the tallest mountain in the realm. It was a moment etched in the memories of all present, including esteemed witnesses like Yawkan, Zaveitth, and the entire assembly of two hundred of our esteemed companions known as Magnusteers.

It was here that Lucus showed his true colors to everyone present. He drew his sword out and went towards my mother. Only twelve years old, I pulled out the sword that was gave me by Zaveitth. I stepped in front of my mother with my sword in a defensive pose. Lucus thrust his sword on top of mine with a loud clanging noise. What I never saw coming was that one of our Magnusteers was on Lucus's side. I heard the Magnusteer tell my mom that if she didn't do what she was told, he make her pay. No one talks to my family like that, not on my watch.

I quickly pulled out my short sword, slipping it where my other sword was as I swung around and pushed the guy away from my mother with the very tip of my long, thin blade. In the process, I pushed Lucus off the mountain's edge. My mother quickly yelled my name as I turned around and put both swords away. I leaped off the edge with my arms outstretched towards Lucus. I then put my arms to my sides and sped up to be under Lucus. Turning around to face up at him, I put my arms out to catch him. He land-ed in my arms, and then something interesting happened.

I thought of a place and time I wanted us to be, and we were soon back on the mountaintop peak. Lucus quickly exited my arms and focused all his attention on me. He had his sword at me, telling me that I had to obey since I was only a child and he was an adult. Instead of pulling my swords back out, I talked with him. I asked him why he was doing this and told him peace is always better. The exchange of words between us was tense, yet I stood my ground, determined to uphold my beliefs in the face of adversity. This confrontation marked a pivotal moment in my journey, shaping me into the resilient individual I am today. What transpired at the peak of Olympus was not just a physical confrontation but a clash of ideologies and beliefs. As the tension between Lucus and myself peaked, the echoes of our words reverberated through the mountain, carrying the weight of our convictions. Lucus, driven by his misguided sense of authority, sought to impose his will upon me, underestimating the power of resilience and determination that burned within my young heart.

In that moment of conflict, I realized that true strength does not solely reside in the sharpness of a blade but in the unwavering resolve to stand up for what is right and be kind to others. As our swords remained at a standstill, the air crackling with intensity, I drew upon an inner wellspring of courage and compassion. It was not about overpowering my opponent but finding a common ground, a path towards understanding and reconciliation.

The exchange of words between Lucus and me was a testament to the transformative power of dialogue and empathy. Despite our adversities, I remained steadfast in my belief that peace and cooperation would always prevail over aggression and hostility. This pivotal moment on Olympus marked the beginning of a new chapter in my journey, where conflicts were resolved through swords and forging bonds that transcended differences and embraced unity.

8
The End Is Only A Beginning

I THOUGHT ALL OF this was done since we had traveled far and long into the past. However, when we returned to the proper time and home, all was not well. Things had somehow been changed, turning our familiar home into the property of a stranger named Robbin D Hood. It may sound absurd when said out loud, but the reality was weirder than fiction. The mere act of getting separated from my parents during our time travel had unforeseen consequences. A young girl from that era somehow remembered me and passed down my fictitious name through her family lineage.

Upon our return, the current owner of our home nearly called the police until my sword and name convinced her otherwise. This older woman, now in possession of our house, shared stories that had been handed down through generations in her family. She said King Richard had to flee his kingdom of kindness in time. He found his way here and somehow purchased this land on which the house is now built for some reason. The Sheriff had followed him here, and they built new lives, and both fell in love. Somewhere within the house is an ancient land deed that states the land and everything belongs to me. Well, King Richard knew that we were time travelers.

It was as if fate had intertwined our lives in ways we could not have imagined. To add to the intrigue, a descendant of the Sheriff of Nottingham lived next door, further blurring the lines between past and present. The ripple effect of our time travel had woven a complex tapestry of connections that transcended time itself, leaving us to navigate a reality that was both familiar and foreign at the same time. The complex web of connections that unfolded before us was both mesmerizing and perplexing. As we delved deeper into the history of our home, now owned by Robbin D Hood, we discovered layers of stories intertwined with our own. It was as if the past had reached out to touch the present, blurring the boundaries of time in ways we never thought possible.

The descendant of the Sheriff of Nottingham living next door added another dimension to the already complex tapestry of our lives. The echoes of the past reverberated through the present, creating a sense of deja vu that was botie and fascinating. The threads of fate seemed to weave us together with these individuals in a dance of destiny that defied rational explanation. This family found clues and facts that can boldly back up the claim that the neighbor, whose last name is Nottingcus, is a direct descendant of Lucus from the Lucusion empire, which explains why he did what he did back in Nottingham.

As we navigated this newfound reality, we realized that our journey through time had not only altered our lives but also left an indelible mark on those around us. The stories passed down through generations are now intertwined with our own, creating a narrative transcending time and space. In this strange and surreal landscape, we found ourselves with questions of identity, belonging, and the true nature of fate.

I plan to recount more of my time travel journeys very soon. Maybe even tell you of the new ones that happen daily; not all are through time. Some are, as many people call them, ordinary every-day events. So hang on tightly to what you've been taught and never choose the side of bad. Always be honest in all your dealings with others, including your parents and teachers, because all of us are making either a legend or a bad person of ourselves.

Definitions of Ancient Tuathain

HYAWA - why

I - I

Uyo - you

Er- are

Veo - love

Em - me

Mhia - him

Rhei - her

Odgo- good

Dab - bad

Ilvg - evil

Cepea - peace

Dirafa - afraid

Keaw -   weak

Prwa -   war

Tlebat -   battle

Einwa -   win

Thrae -   Earth

Gandr(s)-   dragon(s)

Hitewa-   white

Entcian(s)-   ancient(s)

Atrea-   great

Derlea-   victory

Milyfaa -   family

Bybaa-   baby

Irlgat-   girl

Oybt-   boy

Sia-   is

Aybaa-   day

Igtnaa-   night

Fteroonan-   afternoon

ndofua -   found

Hitewa-   white

Entcian(s)-   ancient(s)

Atrea-   great

Derlea-   victory

Milyfaa -   family

Bybaa-   baby

Irlgat-   girl

Oybt-   boy

Sia-   is

Aybaa-   day

Igtnaa-   night

Fteroonan-   afternoon

ndofua -   found

Eepsla-   sleep

Kewaa-   wake

Stera-   rest

Rseaa(s)-   ears

Anglapla-   minute

Oselo -   loose

Oseoch -   choose

Osech -   chose

Ongtrs -   strong

Ryve -   very

Neyho -   honey

Aseleep-   please

Lphea -   help

Edne -   need

Mai -   am

Nca -   can

Otna -   not

Oda -   do

Istha -   this

Nyaa - any

Remo - make

Onpua - upon

Uthmo- mouth

Ona- no

Esyay- yes

Puaua- up

Reaut- are

ritsspi- spirits

LLIwa - will

Tgea - get

Steraf - faster

Werlosa - slower

orema - more

dinfa - find

atati - it

Dragaon Flyiers- Pilots that were chosen to fly futuristic fighter planes made of spliced Dragon DNA and could speak Ancient Tuathain and speak mentally with each other and dragons.

The 21st dimension- The 21st dimension is one that you can see, hear, and still.

Interact with other known dimensions. The universal laws allow you to go back and forth between the 21st and all other dimensions known to exist.

Ghost human(s)- These are super rare and can be dated back to the most ancient of times. They are feared because they are very unpredictable creatures. It is impossible to see them before they attack unless they want you to be able to see them.

Derbwarey: These fantastic, delightful mythical creatures are both male and female. Meanwhile, female derbwarey can be found predominantly hanging around in older buildings. These creatures are the ones to try and see if you need to know something or find another being of any sort. They have been around since the dawn of time and were brought into the state of being to be our guides if we ever get lost.

Celestra castle: Built into a mountainside side, it had two gates, one big enough to fit a Dragaon fighter through and the other just big enough for a single being to walk through that was kept locked with no noticeable ways of unlocking it. Celestra castle is on the seventh plane of existence, or easier said; it's in the seventh dimension. It's also the home of the very Ancient Tuathains.

Dragatha fire guns are shaped like griffins and dragons. They shoot both dragon fire breath and hard round shaped iron that contains black powder.

Marlanaveth: She was and is an Ancient Tuathain and changeling who helps and guides Kloth-ee as a Dragaon Fighter. She also brings a whole new story with her as she travels through time and space. She is also the same person Merlin from the King Arthur stories, but instead of being the man everyone has heard about, she is really a woman. Her age is unknown; she has never talked about it, nor will she do something with her magic for you.

Yawkan: Female leader of the Ancient Tuathain. She is also the birth mother of Dean. While Linda and Stan raised him, they are his guardians.

Definitions of
Peace Giveian

Quins- Equivalent to an Earth city block.

Dlang- Equivalent to one Earth yard.

Wlangs- Equivalent to one Earth foot.

Tas- Equivalent to one Earth inch.

Ageng- Equivalent to one Earth year.

Ang- Equivalent to one Earth hour.

Plangs- Equivalent to one Earth minute.

Pla(s)- Equivalent to one Earth second.

Quakers- These are followers.

Kathal- This is a mighty battle.

Riocard- This means they are an influential leader and powerful rulers.

Lughaidh- Meaning famous warrior.

Gothraigh Tibbot- Meaning strong for the people.

Time diving- This is like dumpster diving or wasting one's time.

Dragatude- When a dragon or dragon-like creature gives you unwanted, disliked, unkind, or mean behavior in the form of body language or tone of voice. Since dragons tend sometimes to have a nasty way of dealing with people and other creatures most of the time.

Mommaude- A term created by Elizaveth Magnus in the year 1877. This is like having an attitude or being rude in response to someone else, except that it is from a mom or mother figure.

Laws of Time Travel

LAW OF NON-INTERFERENCE

- It is strictly forbidden to alter the course of events in the past that could potentially impact the future timeline.

Law of Temporal Anchors

- All time travelers must have a designated temporal anchor to ensure a safe return to their original timeline.

Law of Preservation

- Historical artifacts and events must be preserved in their original state to maintain the integrity of the timeline.

Law of Paradoxes

- Any actions that could create paradoxes or contradictions in the timeline are prohibited.

Laws of Time Travel contin

Law of Temporal Guardians

- Time travelers must uphold their duty as guardians of time, protecting its sanctity and preventing unauthorized temporal incursions.-

Law of Time Loops

-Time loops must be carefully monitored and controlled to prevent infinite recursion and potential damage to the timeline.

Law of Alternate Realities

- Exploration of alternate realities is allowed under strict supervision to avoid cross-contamination with the primary timeline.

Law of Temporal Healing

- Time travelers are responsible for correcting temporal anomalies and restoring balance to disrupted timelines.

Law of Temporal Records

- Accurate and detailed records of all temporal journeys must be maintained for future reference and analysis.

Law of Temporal Ethics

- Time travelers must adhere to a strict code of ethics governing their interactions with past and future individuals to prevent unintended consequences.- Law of Temporal Paradoxes

- Avoid creating paradoxes by interfering with past events that could lead to contradictory outcomes.

Law of Temporal Nexus

- Recognize significant temporal nexus points and exercise caution when making decisions that could alter their course.

Law of Temporal Guardians

- Designate individuals responsible for safeguarding the integrity of the timeline and enforcing temporal laws.

Law of Temporal Research

- Conduct thorough research before planning time travel missions to minimize unforeseen consequences.

Law of Temporal Oversight

- Establish regulatory bodies to oversee and regulate time travel activities to prevent misuse and maintain temporal stability.- Law of Temporal Ethics

- Uphold ethical standards when engaging in time travel activities to ensure respect for historical events and individuals.

Law of Temporal Consequences

- Acknowledge that every action in the past can have ripple effects on the present and future, necessitating careful consideration of choices.

Law of Temporal Limitations

- Recognize the limitations of time travel technology and refrain from attempting to alter events beyond the scope of feasibility.

Law of Temporal Preservation

- Preserve the natural flow of time by refraining from unnecessary interference in historical events, allowing for the organic progression of timelines.

Law of Temporal Unity

- Strive to maintain unity across temporal realities by avoiding actions that could lead to divergent timelines and fragmentation of the time-space continuum.

Recipes

Nectar of the Tuatha

Party Punch

1 each frozen orange juice and

pineapple

1 of each spirit and ginger ale

1 lime sherbet

Single serving drink

1 Lime wedge

2 oz pineapple syrup or juice

1 ½ squirt Blood Orange syrup

1 ½Sprite

1 1/2 ginger ale

Single serving drink

1 Lime wedge

2 oz pineapple syrup or juice

1 ½ squirt Blood Orange syrup

1 ½Sprite

1 1/2 ginger ale or 1 1/2 Lemonade

Elements of Health

1 lb Ground Turkey or Beef

1 bag Frozen mixed vegetables

Proportionate to noodles (Sm elbow or shell)

Butter of choice

Directions

Bring Water and Olive oil to a boil

then add noodles.

Cook your meat of choice on medium till lightly brown. Drain any fluids from the skillet, then put them back down and add your seasoning of choice.

Add your noodles of choice and let

them cook or become soft to your liking.

This should take about 20 minutes.

When noodles, meat, and veggies are cooked, drain the noodles and then lather them noodles in the butter of your choice. Then, mix every-thing.

Enjoy your great balanced meal.

Activities

Activities

I NFINITY OF THE BLOODLINES tells of time travel wrapped around possible events through human history. What events do you think are important for future generations to know and learn from?

Kloth-ee and Zaveitth can travel through time by thinking about when and where they want to go. If you could pick any book to take your mind anywhere, what book would you pick and why?

In the book Infinity of the Bloodlines, the characters often talk about family and the things they have done with them. What have you done with your family in the past that you would want to do again and why?

Discussion and Questions

Choices - What makes a choice the right one? Is it because everyone else is making the same choice?

Bullying - Was Lucus a bully for forcing every-one to do what he wanted? Now think about whether your teachers and parents are bullies. Remember what Kloth-ee was taught. Being kind is far better than fighting. Now think, who do you know that is nice even when they could force you to do something you don't want to do?

Did Kloth-ee ever act as a bully? Even when she was going through history? Now think, who do you know that is nice even when they could force you to do something you don't want to do?

Destiny - We are what we help ourselves be. Reading from good books and learning to be good people will help us to be who we hopefully wish to be.

Oracles - Kloth-ee dreams of a hooded woman, but this woman can see the past, present, and future. Why could it be important to see, let alone remember, the past and present to make a good future for ourselves and others?

Is Kloth-ee's future written, or is it what she makes of it?

Talents - We all have a natural talent or gift. Some may be good at singing, writing, playing an instrument, leading, or even playing a sport. Others may excel at always being honest and having an excellent memory to recite a poem from memory, wisdom, and knowledge to choose good over bad things.

Discussion and
Questions

Discussion and Questions

CHOICES - WHAT MAKES a choice the right one? Is it because everyone else is making the same choice?

Bullying - Was Lucus a bully for forcing everyone to do what he wanted? Now think about whether your teachers and parents are bullies. Remember what Kloth-ee was taught. Being kind is far better than fighting. Now think, who do you know that is nice even when they could force you to do something you don't want to do?

Did Kloth-ee ever act as a bully? Even when she was going through history? Now think, who do you know that is nice even when they could force you to do something you don't want to do?

Destiny - We are what we help ourselves be. Reading from good books and learning to be good people will help us to be who we hopefully wish to be.

Oracles - Kloth-ee dreams of a hooded woman, but this woman can see the past, present, and future. Why could it be essential to see, let alone remember, the past and present so that we can make a good future for ourselves and others? Is Kloth-ee's future written, or is it what she makes of it? Is your future written, and can you still make your own choices?

Talents - We all have a natural talent or gift. Some may be good at singing, writing, playing an instrument, leading, or even playing a sport. While others may excel at always being honest, having an excellent memory to tell a poem from memory, wisdom, and knowledge to choose good things over bad things. What talents or gifts do you have?

Acknowledgements

I want to thank my God in the heavens for giving me the talent of writing and my parents for helping me improve and fine-tune it.

My most loving wife, Marie, who means the whole world to me, I give all the credit; she told me I could finish even when my health said otherwise.

To any person who wants to be good and better, I thank you.

About the author

K D McManis is the author of middle-grade books and young adult novels such as The Mystery Files of Arthur Kelsey, The Beginning, Mystery File of Arthur Kelsey Case of the Shiny Orbs, The Legends of Sleepy Tremont and other stories, Infinities Bloodline vol 1, Infinities Bloodline vol 2. He has six children and six grandchildren and lives with his wife, Marie, in a windy town in the Rocky Mountains. His Facebook page talks about all his books, including what is in the works.

Also by

Mystery Files of Arthur Kelsey: The Beginning

Mystery File of Arthur Kelsey: Case of the Shiny Orbs

Legends of Sleepy Tremont and Other Stories

Infinites Bloodline vol 1

Infinities Bloodline vol 2

The Angelic Scripts (ebook)

Coming Soon

Coming Soon

Legends of Sleepy Tremont: Secrets of A Library

Angent Angels

Mystery File of Arthur Kelsey: Case of the Time
Traveling Thieve

Made in the USA
Middletown, DE
26 November 2024

65001243R00109